HOPI TEA

HOPI TEA

A Murder Mystery

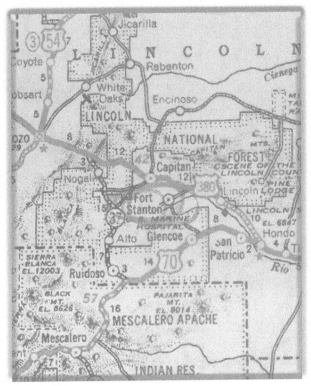

Kent F. Jacobs

SUNSTONE
PRESS

SANTA FE

Sunstone books may be purchased for educational, business, or sales promotional use.
For information please write: Special Markets Department, Sunstone Press,
P.O. Box 2321, Santa Fe, New Mexico 87504-2321.
Cover Artwork › Sallie Ritter
Book design › Vicki Ahl
Body typeface › ITC Benguiat
Printed on acid-free paper
∞
eBook 978-1-61139-534-1

Library of Congress Cataloging-in-Publication Data

Names: Jacobs, Kent, 1938- author.
Title: Hopi tea : a murder mystery / by Kent F. Jacobs.
Description: Santa Fe : Sunstone Press, (2018)
Identifiers: LCCN 2017053141 (print) | LCCN 2017055158 (ebook) | ISBN
   9781611395341 | ISBN 9781632932068 (softcover : alk. paper)
Subjects: LCSH: Border patrol agents–Fiction. | Criminal
   investigation–Fiction. | GSAFD: Mystery fiction.
Classification: LCC PS3610.A356438 (ebook) | LCC PS3610.A356438 H66 2018
   (print) | DDC 813/.6–dc23
LC record available at https://lccn.loc.gov/2017053141

WWW.SUNSTONEPRESS.COM
SUNSTONE PRESS / POST OFFICE BOX 2321 / SANTA FE, NM 87504-2321 /USA
(505) 988-4418 / ORDERS ONLY (800) 243-5644 / FAX (505) 988-1025

For My Sallie

For the wages of sin is death.

—*Romans 6:23*

Cast of Characters

TRACKER DODDS / MR. T: Border patrolmen sent in 1942 to run POW camp at Fort Stanton, New Mexico, the first civilian enemy internment camp in the US prior to the entry of US into WWII. Badly broken leg. Age 50. An ace pilot, former barnstormer. Met J.C. at patrol training camp. Rides an Appaloosa gelding.

KATE MACALLAN: Head nurse at Fort Stanton Merchant Marine Hospital. Age 46. Married twice. Dog named Pluck. Rides a buckskin mare.

J.C.: Jose Chávez, border patrolman. Married to Clara. Two-year old daughter, Linda.

IZZIE JAHATA: Hopi nurse at the Marine Hospital. Crazy, complicated. Loves her tea.

CAPTAIN WILLIAME DAEHNE: Captain of German luxury cruise liner SS Columbus. Scuttled his own ship. 576 survivors became distressed seamen. 410 POW's sent to Fort Stanton.

KLAUS SCHMIDT: Columbus radio operator. Found dead in the swimming pool at POW camp.

GERHARDT MÜELLER: Chef on the Columbus. Now cook at POW camp. Knew Schmidt.

ALBERT GRAFTON: Lawyer, worked for Sen. Fall in Washington, DC. Fluent Spanish. Rancher.

ALBERT BACON FALL: Senator/Secretary of the Interior. Dethroned after Teapot Dome scandal.

PAUL CHINO: Half Apache. Possibly Grafton's son. Mother is Sisika, "Little Bird."

CARL CHINO: Izzie's lover. Half-brother to Paul.

DR. STILLINGTON: Medical-Officer–in-Charge of Merchant Marine Hospital. Built the new hospital for TB patients.

BEAVER: Black patrolman. Cooks for Tracker.

PACO and mother, MARIA: Little boy in bar. Mother was tortured.

CLETIS RODGERS: Owns the Rusty Anchor Bar. Merchant Mariner, had TB.

MARY RODGERS: Married to Cletis. Works in hospital laundry.

PHILLIP ANDERSON: TB patient.

ÁLVAREZ: Lincoln County Clerk. Associated with Grafton.

SHERRIF PATRICK HALLIGAN: Lincoln County Sheriff.

CHIEF VONSHOOVEN -- Border patrol Chief of the El Paso Sector.

LISA BARRÁGON: Wealthy drug lord in Juárez. Poker player.

EVERETT DODDS: Tracker's father.

JUAQUIN: Foreman for Everett Dodds, electrocuted.

HMS HYPERION: British destroyer, attacked the *Columbus*.

USS TUSCALOOSA: American battle cruiser, picked up German survivors.

SS COLUMBUS: German luxury cruise liner caught by outbreak of WWII.

1

Thirty-five mph. Conserve gas, Roosevelt demanded, or he would ration gasoline. The President had already frozen prices last month. Hell, all whiskey distilleries were producing industrial alcohol for torpedo fuel. Housewives saved bacon fat to make glycerin for bombs and bullets. And here he was, putting along a dirt road, driving under 35 to preserve the tires.

"Hey, Tracker. How did you get your name?"

"Pull over."

"We're almost there, Mr. T." A quick glance at the passenger's face. He knew the look.

The jeep skidded to a stop in front of a grassy cemetery filled with neatly rowed crosses. The passenger dragged his leg from the vehicle. He glanced around. Silence. At the entrance to the cemetery, he unbuttoned his fly, began to pee in a broad arc. It was the five Cokes he drank during the interminable drive from El Paso across the desert in 104 degree heat. He enjoyed the moment, the most comfort he had experienced since his release from the hospital.

The plane accident had ended his career as a pilot. And then the Border patrol sent him to the sticks somewhere in the mountains of New Mexico.

A lone rider on a hill above the cemetery watched him. She recognized the border patrol vehicle. The rider pulled a pair of binoculars from her saddlebag, focused on the tall uniformed officer. She could see sweat rings on his tan shirt. She couldn't see much of his face. Dark glasses, aviator-style. Peaked hat, flat brim. He looked fit, well-built. She noticed the crutch.

As he buttoned his fly, he spotted the horse. The rider removed her hat, swept it low like a bow at the end of a performance. A woman. She spun the buckskin mare around and vanished.

He tossed the crutch to the floor, swung his leg into the jeep. He wondered if his driver had seen the woman, but didn't ask. "Let's get going, J.C."

"Your name, sir? All this time we've been working together and I never asked. It's the perfect name for you."

"Tracker? My father named me after his favorite bird dog. I'm not sure if it was meant to be flattering or not. At least he didn't name me after his favorite jackass."

The pea green jeep chugged off, passing a sign on the left—FORT STANTON MARINE HOSPITAL NO. 9—then bumped onto the wooden bridge crossing the Rio Bonito.

■■■

At his desk in the ranch house, Albert Grafton pored over paperwork. Another transfer of title. Ten sections, 6,000 acres. A distressed property due to unpaid taxes. Sold at auction yesterday at the Lincoln County seat in Carrizozo. Grafton was the sole bidder. A smile came across his face. Five cents on the dollar. Damn good for a 60-year-old two-bit lawyer in one of the poorest states in the country.

"This is making me thirsty," Grafton muttered.

"What did you say, Albert?" asked Paul.

Grafton had been a rising star, graduating near the top of his class at the University of Chicago Law School when he was recruited by Fall. At first, he couldn't believe his luck. A hick kid from New Mexico working for a big shot. A senator from New Mexico until President Harding moved him up to Secretary of the Interior. Then Fall blew it. Secretary Albert Bacon Fall had leased Navy petroleum reserves at Teapot Dome in Wyoming and two others in California to private oil companies at low rates. No competitive bidding. A sensational investigation resulted in Secretary Fall being convicted of accepting bribes from the oil companies. Fall was the first Cabinet member to ever go to prison. Almost brought down the oil executives with him. But Grafton helped reduce his time in prison. Indebted, Fall saw that Grafton could grab up prime ranch land back home in New Mexico.

While war raged in Europe, Grafton found a way to make his fortune. He had learned well. He knew every wheeler-dealer in Santa Fe. Self-serving, arrogant bastards. Completely indifferent to wiping out whole families. A nebulous 'ring,' mostly lawyers like himself. Fluent in Spanish. Fluently persuasive in offering to settle Spanish and Mexican land grant controversies, and in return, getting paid with land.

"Sorry, I was just thinking out loud, Paul. Bring me a rum, then get these to Álvarez."

■■■

Paul parked the truck in front of the red brick two-story building, substantial for a small railroad town. Triple-arched entry, balustrade balcony above. The Lincoln County Courthouse. 300 Central Avenue, Carrizozo, New Mexico. County seat and home to the 4th District Court.

His black shoulder length hair hung loose. A red cloth headband sat low on his forehead, keeping his hair out of his eyes. High cheek bones, narrow nostrils, typical of an Apache. A quiet man. A watcher.

"Hey, Paul. Come on in. Been expecting you," said Álvarez.

Paul, deferential as always, nodded in acknowledgement. Went through the swinging door into a small office. He reached into a weathered satchel. Handed the county clerk a raft of legal papers bound in heavy pale blue stock.

"What's the 'House' up to? A new acquisition?" Álvarez closed the Venetian blinds.

"Read the letter," said Paul.

Out loud, Álvarez said, "Willing Guarantor X advanced more than twenty thousand dollars to help the Firm Y to stay afloat. In return, Guarantor received a chattel mortgage. Survey was conducted under the auspices of the Surveyor General, preparatory to the filing of an application with a description of the property that would vest ownership to the claimant." He rifled through the rest of the documents dated June, 1942. "Everything seems to be in order. In a nutshell, X helped out a failing business and loaned them money for which X had a secured debt. Save me some time, Paul. Can you give me a brief description of the property?"

"A store in Nogal. Land, hay, grain, horses. About two thousand head of cattle."

"Water?"

Paul smiled. A rarity for him. "River frontage." A rarity for New Mexico.

"In our fair state, it's all about water. Every precious drop." Paul nodded in agreement. "Okay, it's done. I will record the deed right away. You owe me $18. in filing fees. Best wishes to the 'House,' Paul."

"And to you as well. Good day."

∎∎∎

Kate unsaddled her horse and instructed the stall attendant to wash down and feed the buckskin. She entered the parade grounds in front of the hospital at the exact moment the alarm blared.

Code Zero.

The hospital was filled with mariners from around the globe. All tuberculosis patients. Fort Stanton was an ideal location, Isolated. High altitude, dry air for the most part. And the property was already owned by the government.

Emergencies and deaths were so frequent that Dr. Stillington, the Medical Officer-in-Charge, had long since forbidden the verbal use of Code Zero. The patients knew the designation meant trouble. Big trouble.

Kate wasn't on duty for another two hours, but she ran up the hospital steps. Smelling of horse sweat—but so what.

She heard Dr. Stillington rushing up the cement stairs. She caught the stairwell door before it slammed shut, ran after him. He yelled back to her, "We've got a hemorrhage! Get the pneumothorax cart. And morphine!"

Hair covered, mask in place, gloved, she caught up with him at the bedside of a frantic patient who was clawing his way out of bed. The man had a hand cupped under his chin, trying to catch the stream of bright red blood flowing from his nose. Three other anxious patients looked on. None of them said a word. They all knew what was going on.

With surprising strength, the hemorrhaging patient grabbed Kate's arm and tried to speak. A bolus of blood bubbled from his mouth.

"Don't swallow," said Kate as she caught as much blood as she could with a towel. "Do not swallow."

It took both of them to push the patient back into bed. "Calm down, son," said Stillington. "You're getting something to quiet things."

Philip Anderson tried, but the overpowering sense of choking to death made him panic. To get up. To escape. The tuberculosis germ had eroded a large blood vessel, allowing blood to flood the entire right lung. With each breath he attempted, the pumping action forced blood up his respiratory tree, straight to his mouth.

Kate hurriedly attached long rubber tubes to two single-gallon bottles. Half-filled both with a diluted solution of iodine. She had done the procedure over and over for the past five years. The outcome of spontaneous hemorrhages were fifty-fifty. The patient either recovered or drowned in his own blood.

Stillington held Anderson down. Repeatedly reaching into his mouth to remove a developing bolus of blood. Kate traded places with Stillington, pressing Anderson's shoulders against the bed. Stillington snapped on fresh surgical gloves, opened a white towel-wrapped package, and removed a knitting needle-like instrument on the exposed white enamel tray. Kate lifted the patient's right arm above his head and held it firmly in place.

Stillington rubbed Mercurochrome on the patient's chest, quickly counted down the ribs from the collarbone. Placing an index finger on the eighth rib, middle finger on the seventh of the right side of the chest, he pushed the pneumothorax needle through the skin and intercostal muscle directly between the bones.

Anderson felt a needle prick, then a crunch. Instant stabbing pain.

"Turn the bottles over. Hang them up," said Stillington quietly. He was paying careful attention to the sucking sound. With each attempted breath, air rushed through the open needle. As the patient breathed in, his bad lung deflated, creating a vacuum, pulling air through the pneumothorax needle into the right chest cavity.

Unable to expand against the pressure, the lung collapsed.

Stillington's eyes darted up at Kate, and said as much to himself as to her, "The bleeding is slowing down."

"You're not going to suffocate, Philip." Kate rubbed his forehead with a fresh towel. "Shortness of breath for a bit. Damned SOB. But your other lung will supply plenty of air." The nosebleed stopped. Morphine began to take effect. The swishing sound dropped away.

Dr. Stillington attached the tube to the needle. Checked the bottles. No bubbles. "Looks like we're maintaining air pressure inside the chest cavity. Keeps that lung collapsed."

Stepping away from the bed, Stillington peeled off his mask, hoping he wouldn't have to repeat the procedure. Anderson had enough trouble with the burns on his back. Burns. Deep, denuded, weeping wounds.

"No leakage. Well done, Doctor." With all her experience dealing with TB, from her training in Denver to the registered nursing assignment at Fort Stanton, she knew the patient would most likely survive due to the quick response to the lung compression.

"Have the orderlies move him to the private room downstairs, next to your station. Hypocholorite, sponge the room. Bedding to the steam laundry as usual. I'm going home."

"Yes, sir. If it's alright, I'm heading home. Get a bath. I'm on at eight."

"Of course. Let Izzie know about Mr. Anderson. By the way, where is she, that wild Indian?"

■■■

The jeep followed the Rio Bonito upstream toward a group of temporary buildings facing a 20-acre prison compound secured by barbed wire. No longer a Border patrol pilot, Tracker wasn't happy at all about his new assignment. He was taking charge of a POW internment camp, a bunch of German internees. A work in progress.

"Sheriff's car up ahead," said J.C.

"So?"

"He's your first problem, Mr. T."

Tracker took off his sunglasses, tucked them in the V of his shirt. He had known Jimmy Chávez since he signed up with the Border patrol. When J.C., as he preferred to be addressed, said something, no matter how truncated, he meant it.

A young, pimple-faced guard bolted toward them. "I didn't tell him, J.C. One of the local hired must've said something. He's been..."

J. C. stopped him. "Maxwell, this is the new boss, Senior Patrol Inspector Tracker Dodds."

Tracker touched the brim of his hat, then limped over to the sheriff who was leaning against the hood of his black sedan.

"I'm the Lincoln County Sheriff. Pretty much makes me the head honcho around here."

"I didn't get your name?" Tracker said quietly.

"Everyone knows who I am. Didn't your sidekick there inform you?"

"No."

The sheriff pushed away from the car, moved uncomfortably close. "Sheriff Patrick Halligan. Got it? Sheriff Halligan."

Tracker stepped back, his weight on his good foot. "I'm not deaf, sir. Is there a problem?"

"If you consider a dead man floating in your pool a problem. You've got a corpse in there. A murder, a crime scene, and it's my job to investigate. Do you get it?"

Tracker gave Maxwell a look, a raised eyebrow.

"Sir, he's right," said the guard. "We're in lockdown."

Holy shit. He hurt. Assigned to a job he didn't want. Bone-tired. Needed to pee again. He felt like he was smothering, as if someone had wrapped him in a wool blanket. Pain from top to bottom. His hips, knees. God, he hated getting old.

"What's El Paso thinking? Sending a lame crip?" said Halligan.

Enough. Tracker firmly pushed the sheriff an arm's length away. Tracker was four inches taller than the sheriff and in pretty good shape despite his recently broken limb. He looked down on the sheriff, pushed his hat up a bit, rubbed his greying sideburn. The skin of Tracker's neck was leathery brown. A career spent in the sun. Limited body language from Tracker was making Halligan nervous."Sheriff Halligan, I'm sorry we've started out this way," Tracker said in a tired voice. "This is the Fort Stanton Detention Camp for prisoners of war. You're on federal property. Under the control of the Department of Justice. To refresh your memory, a federal agency isn't under your county jurisdiction."

"Bullshit. There's been a criminal act and my main charge is to keep the peace."

Itching to punch the meddling bastard, he felt like a teacher on playground duty, keeping little bullies from causing trouble. Tracker wanted to say the sheriff was butting in, instead said, "I'm sure there will be times when I'll need your assistance."

Halligan wasn't listening. "I'm going in."

"How do you know it is murder?" asked Tracker.

"You're not going to let me in?"

"You got that right. Now, get off my property."

The sheriff opened the car door. "I'm calling Governor Miles. He'll be glad to tell you who's the boss around here. I'll have your balls on a plate for dinner tonight." Halligan shifted the old Ford in reverse, then shot forward, almost clipping the officers.

An electric strike of pain shot from the base of Tracker's spine to the tip of his big toe. Shooters, he called the pains. He heard J. C. muttering.

"Cabrón. Creo que no."

Tracker laughed. A first for the day.

2

The prison perimeter lights came on. Tracker felt a chill. He breathed in the dank odor of recently poured cement. Four new buildings in progress. Radio room. Showers. Two new barracks for the guards, probably a cot for him somewhere.

Radio antenna mounted on a pole high above on the flat roof of the adobe headquarter building was his contact with the border patrol headquarters in El Paso. Chief Vonshooven was going to love his first report: Nothing much is going on, sir, just a fight with the local authority over custody of, well, sir, a dead man, possibly a murder.

Coiled barbed wire. Rifle barrels protruded from guard towers, glinting silver-white in the powerful lights. Two border patrolmen, guard dogs at their side, swung open the main gate leading into the POW camp. Barracks, whitewashed walls the color of fetid water. Two long rows. German POWs in stained denim overalls. Sunburned. Sullen. Sober.

Tracker ignored the salutes of the prisoners as they walked up the dirt street. "When did you find the body?"

"First round of checks, just a little while ago," answered Maxwell.

"Nothing touched, I hope."

Maxwell led the way up the hill to the floodlit Olympic-sized swimming pool. Tracker blinked. Held out a hand, signaling J. C. to stay back.

The scene before him resembled a grisly black and white photograph, colorless except for a tinge of red. A body floated face down. Clad in overalls, a sodden dark blue. A small pool of blood surrounded the head of the body, gradually staining the water with the vague undulating motion of the pool. No trace of blood on the back of the man's shirt. Not attacked from behind. He walked slowly around the pool to a high diving board on the far side, a better view of the scene.

The top of the man's head had been scalped. Semi-circular cuts on each side of the head just above the ears. A fierce yank had removed the scalp exposing the bare skull. Brutal. Violent. Hideous.

"Jesus!" Tracker breathed.

3

He pointed his crutch at Maxwell. A bad habit. "What was going on in camp when you found him?" Pain shot down his leg. He planted the crutch, raised his bad leg a few inches from the deck.

"The second shift of POWs were in the mess hall for supper. The rest were back in their barracks, sir. "

"Maxwell, rope off the area. Go get a camera. Photograph the scene before we move him." Until now his eyes had been fixed on the body. Tracker methodically walked around the pool, searching the soil just beyond the deck. No evidence of a scuffle. No evidence of the body being dragged to the pool. Occasional footsteps in the dusty soil. He followed several paths and all appeared to lead down toward the dirt strip separating the barracks. No sign someone had run away. He pointed to a small building at the north end of the Olympic-sized pool, and signaled J. C. to circle around the other side. A bleached canvas awning covered the deck at that end. Tracker skirted the benches underneath. Withdrew his pistol.

J. C. ducked around the concrete tower supporting the high diving board. Pressed against the building entrance. At Tracker's signal, he kicked the door open, stepped inside. Flipped the light switch. "All clear—just cleaning supplies, brushes, hoses. Chemical stuff."

Tracker took a look, turned back to the floating body. Water lapped quietly in the wide gutters at the lip of the pool.

"A tall guy," he mumbled. "Athletic build. He would have put up a fight—someone must have heard something."

Maxwell knelt nearby and leaned forward with a camera. Flashbulbs popped. The air smelled like molten glass. He asked Tracker a question, but Tracker wasn't listening.

Tracker was in his element. An instructor at the border patrol training camp told him that some agents *see* a memory like a movie, others *have* the memory. It takes nuanced mental focus to absorb all the data.

"That's enough," Tracker said to Maxwell. "Get the prisoners in formation. Take roll call. J. C., fish the guy out. I want a closer look."

J. C. removed his boots, pistol, holster, everything but his boxers, climbed down the ladder and slipped into the water. He swam to the body, locked an arm around the prisoner's neck and underarm, kicked for the edge. Grunting with effort, he lifted the torso out of the water. Tracker dropped his crutch and grabbed the dead man's arms, unceremoniously dragging the body through the gutter on to the deck. Leveraging himself on the pool's edge, J. C. sprung out of the pool. Together they rolled the body over.

Opaque eyes were wide open. Skin a waxy white. The fringe of remaining blond hair slowly turned red at the site of the scalping.

"Recognize him?" Tracker asked.

"Not sure, sir. He's tall, blond, probably used to be blue-eyed. Hitler's ideal, wouldn't you say, Mr. T?"

Tracker nodded in agreement. His attention was on the gradually widening red ring on the man's shirtfront. He stooped, supporting his weight on the crutch, unbuttoned the shirt, fully expecting a bullet hole or some sort of gash. Only a small puncture wound. In fact, were it not for the oozing blood at first glance, he might have missed it. "Post guards. Light's about gone. We'll have to search the area in the morning."

His right leg was one electric flame of pain. He had bent it unnaturally, made it do work it wasn't ready to do. Largest bone in the body. Multiple fractures. Also shards left by crush injuries. A femoral transverse fracture takes four-to-six months to heal. He was barely four months post-surgery. He was in no condition to do any questioning now, and he knew it. "Have the senior German officer in my office first thing in the morning."

"Sir!" called Maxwell, walking swiftly towards them. "Your corpse is Seaman Klaus Schmidt."

My corpse, Tracker thought with a grimace. "Before the prisoners are dismissed, get all of Schmidt's belongings, strip his bed. Everything to my office." Tracker turned to J. C., asking, "I do have an office..." He caught J. C.'s nod. "Get a truck up here. I sure as hell can't help carry him out."

"Got it, Mr. T."

4

"I'm taking a break, Izzie," Kate whispered, "Watch Mr. Anderson. He's still critical." That odd, remote look was back in Izzie's eyes.

Walking out the front doors, she heard tires crunching on the gravel road behind the hospital. She stepped around the side of the building in time to see a pickup with wood sideboards turn the corner and come to a stop. Tracker stepped down from the passenger side of the cab. Maxwell jumped from the back.

In the light of the service entrance, she recognized the driver and called out, "J. C., what've we got?"

Before Chávez could answer, Tracker said, "Is the doctor in?"

"No, but I can call him. J.C., are you and Clara settled in?"

"Please call the doctor." Tracker's face was expressionless, his speech clipped. He was fighting to control the pain. Godamnit.

"Do I have a patient or don't I?"

"You do. A dead one."

"I'll determine that," Kate said flatly.

"Believe me, he's dead. Take a look." Tracker flipped back a sheet covering the body.

Kate bit her lip. "He's been scalped," said Tracker, his voice had no inflection.

"I can see that." Sepia photos she had seen as a little girl in Wyoming in her father's office flashed through her mind. The image of channeled faces of two Indian chiefs, standing like bronze statues beside a string of scalps. Most impressionable to a six-year-old. As if thinking out loud, she said, "The Sioux scalped their enemies with the head attached. My father said it was the ultimate sign of victory."

Tracker ignored her comment. "They'll bring it in."

"Take him directly downstairs to the morgue. You're not going to upset my patients." Kate walked ahead, opened the stairwell door leading to the basement. J. C. and Maxwell maneuvered the stretcher down the tight stairwell and transferred the body on to the metal table.

The corpse's features were swollen, grossly distorted. "Do you have any idea who he is?" Kate asked. "I am told Klaus Schmidt," said Tracker.

"One of the guys from the *Columbus*," J. C. added.

"I thought I recognized him," said Kate. "He worked in the stables. Spoke passable English."

Tracker took off his hat, ran a hand through his hair. Kate noticed the shadow of his beard was as grey as his hair. A moth circled in the light of the surgical lamp and dove through the space between them. Neither blinked.

"Can you get the doctor?" Tracker asked.

"It's late. He's at home, probably sitting down to dinner. This can wait until morning."

"I need an autopsy tonight."

"He's not going anywhere tonight or tomorrow. I certainly don't appreciate your callousness at the taking of a human life. Exactly who are you?"

"Look, I was sent up here to run the camp and this had just happened." He reached out to offer his hand. "Senior Patrol Inspector Dodds, Tracker Dodds."

Kate ignored his hand. "Well, Mr. Dodds, you're certainly on a short fuse."

"I need to know..."

"You'll get the doctor's report when it's ready." She brushed past him.

...

Maxwell showed Tracker the only available room. It was the size of a closet, but at least it was private. A cot. Wash bowl. Small cracked mirror. A bare light bulb. His duffle and book bag were by the narrow bed. He collapsed on the cot. His crutch clattered to the wooden floor and he couldn't have cared less.

A bell rang out. He checked his pocket watch. The goddamned bell had rung every half hour since he arrived. The sailors from the *Columbus* were maintaining a shipshape routine, behind barbed wire or not. Tracker had been told things were more strict since the arrival of Nazis. Cyclone fences reinforced, floodlights panned the camp all night. Curfews were enforced, lights out at ten o'clock. Dog patrol on duty 24/7.

His welcoming committee included an arrogant sheriff, a brutally mutilated body and a pissed-off nurse. He was good at reading people. Eyes. Hands. Body language. His chief had commented on Tracker's lack of body language, which disconcerted a lot of people. Especially when you were interrogating someone. When Vonshooven asked him why he was so unflinching, he had told the chief the truth. When you grow up with an alcoholic father, you learn to keep everything inside. Plan ahead. Know the exits. Have an excuse. Duck. Stay alive. When trapped, shut up and take the whipping. Get out of sight. Tracker couldn't shut his father out, but he could disappear. His mother smuggled books to him. She was his savior; they were his escape route.

Unable to sleep, he tried to read, but ended up staring at the ceiling. He realized he must have slept when the smell of coffee awakened him. Rising stiffly on the crutch, he slowly transferred weight to the weak leg, withered, and pearl-white from the cast. As blood rushed to his foot, he muffled a curse. Poured water from a pitcher over his head. Dipped his straight edge razor in the basin, managed a cursory shave. Uniform trousers, fresh shirt. SPI badge, leather chest strap, collar insignias in place. Dark tie. He glanced at his un-emptied duffle bag, pushed it under the cot with his crutch. "That can wait," he muttered, realizing he hadn't eaten since leaving El Paso.

In the kitchen, which also served as the dining room, he was greeted by a patrolman standing over the stove. "Beaver's my name, sir. Want some coffee?"

Tracker grunted. Sat down at the chrome-legged white linoleum-topped table. Took several napkins from the chrome dispenser. "You have a first name?"

"That's it, sir, Beaver," he said, setting down a thick-lipped white ceramic mug in front of Tracker. "That's my whole name. I stay real busy and can build about anything. I'll be taking care of you like my family, and I LOVE my family." Beaver was black, with a ring of white fuzz on his head. Large green eyes. Sculpted nose. He was big, trim, looked strong, but was beat up.

"How long have you been with the border patrol? You look as old and decrepit as me."

Beaver laughed. Low and mellow. "I served at the Last Supper, sir. No, honestly, my Mother was Mexican, so what does a black man do when all he knows is how to fight, shoot, and is bilingual—join the border patrol. I just don't have much tread left on my tires."

"Me neither. Makes sense to me. Been here long?"

"Since the *Columbus* crew arrived."

"I was briefed." The German crew found themselves in the wrong place at the wrong time. Chief Vonshooven told him Germany had gone to war during their last Caribbean cruise. December, 1939.

1939. That was before the accident that landed him in the hospital. The doctors at William Beaumont Hospital in El Paso told him his chance of a career in the Army Air Corps was nil. He could never pass the physical. Sitting in the churning whirlpool in the rehab center, the steam covered his reaction to the white-coated gods standing not five feet from him. The medical professionals talking about him as if he couldn't hear. He went on the biggest drunk of his life that night.

"How do you like your eggs?"

"Uh." Tracker shook his head, clearing his mind. "Over easy."

Beaver pried the lid off a blue tin, scooped out a dollop of lard and plopped it in a cast- iron skillet. Over the sizzling sound, he said, "I will do my very best, sir."

As the chief said, the *Columbus* wasn't technically a military ship, but the captain had no choice but to obey orders from the German High Command to run the British blockade and get back to Germany ASAP. When they did make a break for it, that is, attempt to leave neutral waters, a British destroyer, the *HMS Hyperion*, was on them in a heartbeat. Captain Daehne ordered the *Columbus* scuttled. In a well-rehearsed drill, he abandoned his ship after opening the seacocks and setting her on fire. Luckily for the Germans, the *USS Tuscaloosa*, an American cruiser, was nearby. The Americans picked up 576 survivors. The Fed at Ellis Island labeled them as distressed seamen.

The sailors became prisoners of war.

Beaver brought him a plate of two eggs, refried beans, fried Spam, and a stack of warm flour tortillas. "More coffee?"

Tracker nodded, bit into a tortilla. "Where're you getting coffee?"

"From the prisoners. They get packages from Germany. How do you like that? We trade pork for coffee. The ship's cook makes damn good sausage."

"Have a seat. Got any salsa?"

"This is all I got."

A bottle of Tabasco appeared. Beaver sat, took a swallow of coffee. "The German government sends each of them three dollars a month—maritime law."

"I didn't know that. Sounds like they're better off than a lot of people around these parts." Tracker smothered his eggs in hot sauce, pushed frijoles into the mix, took a huge bite. Woofed the tortilla.

"How did you sleep?"

"Goddamn bell," said Tracker.

Beaver laughed, a deep resonating laugh, with a grin from ear-to-ear. He carried the empty plate to the sink, slid it into the dishpan. "I may have to remove that clapper."

"I'll be in my office. When J. C. comes in, tell him I want to see him. And get on the radio to El Paso, dispatch my report on last night's incident to Chief Vonshooven."

"Yes, sir."

Tracker opened the door to his office. Regulation wooden desk. Requisite photo of Franklin Delano. Wooden file cabinet. Empty gun case. Swivel desk chair with a cracked green leather seat. Two straight-backed chairs pushed against the wall.

Even at 5:30 in the morning, the room was stuffy. He pushed open the shutters, glanced out. In the half-light just before dawn, the shadows were deep violet. A sliver of moon hung in the pale sky. A slight breeze. Tightness in his jaw lessened. He chewed an aspirin. Swallowed coffee.

A narrowing valley lay before him, upland slopes covered with piñon, juniper and scrub pine, all casting long shadows. Beyond loomed Sierra Blanca, its northeastern face absorbing the first pink light as the sun tipped over the horizon.

He spotted a rider on a distant hill, a perimeter guard on the early shift. Even at this distance, he could tell the man in the saddle was a pro. Reins in one hand, rifle in the other. It had been a long time since he had thought of riding horseback, much less for pleasure. He blamed his father for this, as he blamed him for so many things. Maybe all the hatred was partly his own stubborn fault, but he just couldn't bring himself to give an inch to the bastard.

▪▪▪

After that disastrous controlled-burn years ago at the ranch in Kansas, Tracker and his father had returned in silence to the barn. Everett Dodds showed no emotion whatsoever over his foreman's horrific death. The spring burn meant to promote new growth had accomplished just the opposite. Sparked by the out-of-control flames, an arc of high-voltage electricity had exploded, driving straight into Juaquin's body below. Blackened hands left clutching his throat, tortured face mostly gone. Unrecognizable. Juaquin, a good man, taking on anything Everett asked even though that lame leg must have always been killing him. Even as a kid, Tracker had tried to do what his father asked, but it was never enough. How old was he when he had realized that Everett Dodds was just plain mean?

When that man had turned around and stared at him, standing barely twenty feet away, Tracker had thought his father was going to tell him how sorry he felt about the death. Oh no, instead, he had raised his voice, ranting wildly on about how Juaquin had let the burn get out of hand, that Juaquin's death was his own damn fault.

Back at the barn, Tracker had lost control, just lost it. He didn't remember exactly what caused him to snap. He grabbed a crowbar hanging on the wall. Threw that mother as hard as he could, missing his father's head by inches.

He never saw him again.

Tracker was sixteen. He had packed his few belongings, gone into the kitchen, and told his mother that 'Bad weather's coming.' It was their code-talk, meaning Everett Dodds was coming her way. He saw himself in the kitchen, white cabinets in need of paint after years of her scrubbing. Had she scrubbed down to bare wood to cleanse, or to wipe away her husband's withering insults and beatings? Everett Dodds had become a gruesome, despicable person.

Panic in her eyes, her thin hands clutched at him, begging him not to leave her. He knew she could read his mind. Her face contorted with emotion, tears flowing, but she could not speak. She fell to her knees, and with difficulty, she reached out to him once more.

From that moment, his life had turned upside down. He knew he would kill his father if he stayed one more second. He could not help her. He bolted out the back door, her pitiful screams ringing in tortuous pain.

■■■

Tracker blinked, returning to the present. Swallowed his grief. Grief and regret eroded his entire being. It was eating him up, like acid eating through steel, corrosive and ruinous. He shut his eyes tightly, willing the memory to vanish.

Wearily, he slouched down in the desk chair, stretched out his leg. He found three ledgers in the center drawer. On top, an inventory of the former Conservation Corps Camp. Roosevelt's attempt to provide jobs during the Great Depression. A positive, but not perfect solution. That old compound was the predecessor to the prisoner of war camp. The land belonged to the U.S. government, miles from nowhere. A perfect solution.

There were six barracks, kitchen, mess hall. Communal latrines, lavatory, a shower block.

He glanced out the other window of the corner office. The internment camp was in full view. Calisthenics were underway. The Germans were organized and energetic. Despite a brutal murder in their ranks, no one seemed to falter. Routine, he reminded himself, can erase a lot of things. He spotted Beaver sawing a two-by-four with the vigor of his namesake.

There was a rap on the door. *"Buenos días*, Mr. T. Sleep much?"

"Some, I guess. Have a seat."

"You know, in case that sheriff..."

"Screw the sheriff. Get down to business."

"Right. Okay, we know the victim is Seaman Klaus Schmidt."

"Was..." Tracker said as he fingered a steno-pad on the desk. "Schmidt have any obvious enemies? A revenge killing? Was there a motive or motives?"

"Had a fight with a new prisoner not long ago."

"Fill me in."

"We'd just gotten twenty more, all Nazis. Schmidt was no Nazi, at least he didn't show it."

Underneath the ledger, Tracker found the leather-bound log taken from Captain Daehne. A total of 410 men had been shipped by train to New Mexico. The female crew and men under seventeen were sent back to Germany via Japan, and a few had gotten away while temporarily held on Angel Island near San Francisco. It still wasn't clear to Tracker who decided to send the Germans to Fort Stanton, or why the border patrol was put in charge.

It really didn't matter to him. It was his job, a paycheck.

He remembered Chief Vonshooven coming down pretty hard on him. The chief wasn't going to let a little self-doubt ruin a talented, dedicated professional that he himself had trained.

Vonshooven's parting words were crystal clear. "Got your old side-kick to drive you up there, fill you in. Tracker Dodds, don't screw up. You blew your chance to fly. You're alive. Touch your heart. You're alive."

Tracker focused on his sidekick, asking, "So none of these men from the ship are Nazis?"

"I don't think so, more like really nationalistic."

"I saw a truck leave as we were talking to the sheriff."

"I checked. Albert Grafton, rancher. Like I told you on the drive up here, we do business with him—pork, beef."

Tracker's briefing was extensive.

U. S. MARINE HOSPITAL, No. 9, FORT STANTON, NEW MEXICO
150 miles Northeast of El Paso. Altitude 6,235'
92 bed hospital built in 1938. Full capacity 242 beds
+ 75 two-bed open-air tents for ambulatory patients

Tracker had been told Fort Stanton was one of the only sanatoriums that accepted 'far-advanced' patients, meaning those with severe hemorrhagic fevers, diarrhea and emaciation. Their greatest fear was contagion. Vonshooven read him the grim stats from 1940. Twenty-five per cent died in hospital. Projected that 50% of patients released would die within five years.

Mighty lousy odds. He took a deep breath, turned back to the inventory.

Latest X-ray, radio phones for each bed.
Fluoroscopic apparatus. Surgical suites main floor.
Elevator (the first in NM).
Occupational therapy building.

The Fort is essentially self-sufficient, Tracker thought. It has to be. Remote, high, dry.

"Walk me around later, give me the stats now."

"Yes, sir. Pretty much a small town. There's a power and regenerating plant. Electrical and water distributing plants. One-million-gallon concrete reservoir. Steam laundry. Maintenance crews for everything. They live in dormers by those clay tile silos you saw when we drove by. Fire department. Dairy. Mechanic. Barns. Abattoir, our own butcher."

Tracker saw the livestock counts: Cattle herd 779. Hogs 393. Corrals 59 horses.

J.C. told him there was a landing strip for small aircraft nearby. A motion picture theater. Two churches. Even a Seaman's Social Club. No response from Tracker.

"Mr. T, you alright? That leg bothering you?"

"I'm fine. This is quite an operation. I'm impressed. You mentioned a landing strip?"

"Yes. Doctors fly in from Albuquerque. Specialists." J. C. leaned forward in the straight-backed chair. "Breakfast okay?"

"Yeah."

"Beaver's a damn good cook. Wait 'til you taste his soda biscuits smothered in Mormon gravy."

Tracker didn't hear him, his mind leaping ahead, his concentration solely on the problem. "Sum total of what we've got so far. One dead man. German. Scalped. A small hole in his belly. Very little blood from either wound. That kind of surprised me. One visitor in the camp at probable time of death -- Grafton. Internees were either eating or in their quarters. So far no one in the group stands out as an enemy or whatever." He stabbed the pencil hard on the paper. "Damn, we need that autopsy report. Let's head over to the hospital, give a little goose to the process," Tracker said, reaching for his crutch. "What's the name of that nurse we saw last night?"

•••

Dr. Andrew Stillington stepped back from the autopsy table, his mask hiding a perplexed grimace. He knew he was as good a physician as anyone in the state of New Mexico. However, even though it was before 7 am, Stillington felt the familiar immobilizing effect of depression building in him. He reached into his lab coat pocket, pulled out a thin silver flask. He pushed down the mask, swallowed the bourbon-flavored water. He traced his finger over the engraving on the flask.

"Dr. Stillington?" called J.C., holding the door open for Tracker who was coming down the steps one at a time. "This is Patrolman Agent Dodds, Doctor."

"Welcome, gentlemen. A pleasure to meet you, Agent Dodds." The doctor had a pleasant southern accent.

"Tracker, please sir."

"A most hideous occurrence. I assume you know that he was scalped—crudely scalped. Have you found it?"

"Found what?"

"The integument of the upper part of the head, including the associated subcutaneous structures—the scalp."

"No, we haven't found it."

"It's the proof of killing—important to the killer."

"A trophy. But that wasn't the cause of death, was it?"

Stillington looked up over his reading glasses at Tracker and raised his eyebrows. "You are correct. His neck was broken. Probably the killer used his head for leverage when he scalped him." The doctor pulled a Buck skinner knife from his pocket and snapped it open with one hand. The blade angled downward, with a more blunt point making it harder to make an accidental slice. "Like this." He stepped behind J. C., wrapped an arm tightly around his neck, and with a whoosh, swept the skinner through the air an inch above J. C.'s head.

J. C. exhaled. Tracker smiled and said, "Interesting." Thinking to himself that was probably the biggest reason that white men look at Native Americans as subhuman heathens.

Stillington folded the lockback shut. "But the weapon wasn't very sharp—the scalp wasn't a clean cut—more like it was gouged out of the skull. There was also a puncture wound in the upper belly, caused by something slightly bigger than an ice pick, something similar to a stiletto."

"And?" Slow down, let the man talk, Tracker reminded himself. He had learned that silence is as important as restraining body language. He blinked. He saw himself listening to his father.

▪▪▪

Tracker had never seen Everett Dodds act like that in his life. His father was laughing, performing like a master of ceremonies, front and center in a circus, hawking his attractions, extremely animated. Singing, chortling. Cracking jokes that weren't funny. Everett had lunged forward and slugged his wife in the face, spun her around and began choking her.

Wise to the moods of his father at the age of fifteen, Tracker knew to slow down. Instead of beating the shit out of his father, he calmly poured a glass of whiskey and handed it to him. When Dodds took the drink, his wife dropped limply to the floor. Tracker scooped her up and carried his mother away. His father seemed to have lost interest in them. He was humming and drinking. Humming and drinking.

▪▪▪

Stillington fingered his goatee, cleared his throat. Tracker was back, focused. "When I opened the belly, it was full of blood. That's why so little bleeding came from the scalp wound. The poor devil had already bled out."

"Wait a minute, just how long would it take to bleed that much? To entirely fill the belly?"

"Half an hour, give or take a little depending on the size of the blood vessel injury."

"Umm. So he was scalped later. Right?"

"An assumption. A very smart assumption if I can prove it." The phone on the wall rang and Stillington stepped away, turning his back on the two patrolmen.

The ghoulish surroundings of the morgue were nothing new to Tracker. He was familiar with those in El Paso. This one was just smaller. A saccharine, sweet smell of filtered air filled his nostrils as a large wall fan oscillated rhythmically. Everything was as neat and tidy as Dr. Stillington's immaculately trimmed goatee. It always bothered Tracker how devoid of humanity a morgue seemed. Pristine white walls, no ornamentation. Highly waxed floor, a single shiny, cold, stainless steel table with a brilliant light above. A scale hanging from the ceiling where each organ was weighed after being removed from the various cavities of the corpse.

The difference between this corpse and those Tracker had seen in El Paso was the citizenship of the body that lay in front of him. Not a Mexican alien, but a German, a man of similar height and build as Tracker himself. He wondered what the man could have possibly done to inspire such an act of mutilation. Scalping took not only strength but also an aboriginal appetite. A vicious, animalistic act. Tracker was repulsed.

The phone clicked as Stillington hung up.

"The puncture weapon had to have caught something pretty big," Tracker said.

"It did," Stillington replied. "As I suspected, the abdominal aorta. All the way to his spine. The killer really drove that weapon deep. But something else is really bothering me.

There's no sign of clotting anywhere. Internally or externally. That doesn't make sense. I've sent blood and bone marrow samples up to the state lab in Santa Fe for tests."

"How long will that take?"

"A few days—I put STAT on the order. Why don't you come around later this afternoon, maybe I'll have more for you then."

"Doctor, are you are hunter? The Buck knife?"

"Goodness, no. It was my fathers. I've always carried it with me. If you'll excuse me, gentlemen, I have work to do." Stillington also needed another nip. "You're welcome to examine the body."

5

"Notice anything, Mr. T?"

"I smelled it, too. Head on back, J. C., start a search for a weapon. A stiletto, something thin, very sharp. And bring that ship captain to my office. I'll be there in a half hour," Tracker said, turning toward the front entrance to the hospital.

"Right, Mr. T."

A nurse outside Ward 1 watched him approach. He placed his flat-brimmed hat on the counter and introduced himself. "And you are?"

She looked straight through him but made no reply. Tracker wondered if she heard a word he said.

Kate emerged from the adjacent ward, carrying a tray of sputum specimen bottles. "Mr. Dodds. Thought that was you. Izzie, I'll take over. You need to head up the hill and check on the ambulatory patients."

"About last night..." He paused. She was definitely checking him out. (Had he forgotten to button his fly?)

She put the specimens in the ice box, then picked up a stack of clipboards, patient charts attached. "Anything new on Mr. Schmidt?"

"No." Tracker waited for her to turn around. She didn't. "You said you knew the prisoner?"

"A little. He was sick when he first arrived. We kept him several days. Later they put him to work in the stables."

His first good look at her confirmed what he remembered from the night before—she was dark-haired, fair-skinned. Her short hair was cropped in a wedge, almost tomboyish. Most women wore their hair in a pageboy, the ends curled under, and each hair in place, like a helmet. Her only jewelry was a plain chain securing her ID badge.

When she finally turned to look at him, he took his time. He also was good at being silent. So he was surprised to hear himself ask, "Do you have time for a break?"

Unblinking, and giving nothing away, she said, "One cigarette."

Tracker opened the door for her. "You're a little smoother around the edges this morning," Kate said as she exhaled a breath of smoke and bent over to adjust the seam of her white stockings. Straightening up, she held out her cigarette pack. He removed one and lit it with the Zippo she offered. (Why? he wondered later. He didn't smoke.) "So what do you think?" she asked. The expansive parade grounds spread out in grassy triangular sections in front of the hospital.

He hesitated, his mind not on his job, then answered, "I told you we really don't know anything about the murder."

"Not that, what do you think of Fort Stanton?"

"Looks like good ranching country."

At that moment a large black dog with a white ring around one eye and one white foot loped up to Kate. She ruffled the dog's ears and patted his back, for which she received mushy kisses. "Meet Pluck. My best friend and sleeping companion."

Tracker thought she winked at him but wasn't sure. He needed to take the weight off his bad leg, so he asked, "Mind if I sit for a minute?" Right hand on the railing, he lowered himself down on the hospital steps. She joined him. Smoothed her white skirt over her knees. Pluck planted another kiss on her neck.

"I never introduced myself. Kate MacAllan."

"You from around here?" Tracker asked. No answer. He waited and said again, "Grow up here? Family nearby?"

She was on her feet and back inside before he could finish the sentence.

The big dog rubbed against his leg, licked his hand. "Well, Pluck, what the hell have I done now?"

`The nurse called Izzie was standing under a cottonwood tree, her face, as best he could tell, expressionless. He acknowledged her by snapping a brief salute. She took a sip from the mug in her hand, smiled briefly. Walking back down First Street, he noticed a stenciled sign in front of a building centered on the parade grounds. ANDREW STILLINGTON, M.D., MEDICAL OFFICER-IN-CHARGE. A large white stucco house, a screened-in porch, high-pitched green shingle roof. A withered honeysuckle vine clinging to a trellis. Curtains drawn.

As he stepped on to the swinging bridge connecting to the camp, it occurred to him there was very little around him that seemed the least bit friendly. Ninety-two beds, plus seventy-five two-bed tents on the hill, all seriously ill, maybe dying.

■■■

"Bring him in," said Tracker.

"Captain Wilhelme Daehne, sir," J.C. said, stepping back, pressing against the door.

Tracker pulled a chair to the center of the room. The grating sound of the chair legs scraping on the pine floor set the mood. "Have a seat." Tracker remained standing, arms folded across his chest. Took his time walking behind the captain. The man before him was suave, trim, bald-headed. Suave, yes, but tense, which seemed understandable considering he was wearing denim dungarees and a work shirt labeled POW instead of a spiffy naval uniform.

"Are there problems? My men are cooperating, they obey me," said Daehne, not moving.

Tracker walked around the captain to his desk. "You speak very good English, Captain."

"*Norddeutscher Lloyd*, the owners of the *Columbus*, insisted all crew who work with the passengers speak fluent English. The *Columbus* was very popular with Americans."

"Then you will understand everything I say?" The captain nodded. "This man Schmidt, just exactly what did he do?"

"He was my chief radio operator."

"Was he liked?"

"Yes," Daehne said politely.

"I mean was he close to the other crew members?"

"He was certainly liked well enough, but he did tend to be a person who kept to himself."

"By that you mean?" Tracker leaned against his desk.

"He performed his duties diligently. To my knowledge he never had cross words with other crew members. Ate with the others, but he was, what word should I use—a loner. Kept to himself when he wasn't on duty."

Tracker had to admit he was pretty much the same. "Go on, Captain, you wouldn't have mentioned 'loner' if you weren't bothered by it."

"Klaus would often appear in the most unexpected places on the ship. Also, he spent what I considered undue time with passengers."

Tracker thought about the answer. "Do you think he was spying? Something like that?"

"I considered it, however, every single bit of communication crosses my desk, and believe me, he sent no suspicious radio messages. He seemed rarely, if ever, to disembark when we were in port. I'm nearly certain he made no effort to transmit information to anyone."

"Maybe he was storing info up or maybe he hadn't hit a mother lode, so to speak."

"Mother lode?"

"Something really important," Tracker said.

"Ah, I understand. Klaus did nothing to make me confront him or investigate. May I remind you the men from my ship are not Nazis, nor are we soldiers. We are German citizens in an American prison."

"You wouldn't be here if Germany hadn't invaded Poland. Don't bait me. I am not interested in your viewpoint. You are in *my* prison."

Tracker looked out the window facing the camp. Prisoners were raking and chopping weeds in the vegetable gardens near the river. The ship's bell rang. Ten o'clock. Without turning, Tracker glanced at his pocket watch. Time to irritate the bastard. "Two seconds late, Captain."

"Can't be."

Watch in the palm of his hand, he held it up. "A pilot's chronograph. Military specs. Rotating bezel with an arrowhead index. Antimagnetic. Luminescent escapement. And very rugged. Won it in a poker game."

The captain shifted, tapping his feet. A small movement, body language barely noticeable, but to Tracker it was a sign. Was he trying to hide something? The captain didn't like being questioned or challenged. Neither did Tracker.

Tracker considered ways, none of them particularly genius, to get past the stone facade. He could press the patriotic and/or Aryan button, but Daehne had already announced he was no soldier. He could try embarrassing the man, say put him to work in the latrines, or make him pick weeds with his fingers. Anything abhorrent to a man of a high pedigree. But Tracker decided to treat the captain as what he was, a man caught in the middle of a very bad journey.

"J.C., get him out of here."

After dismissing Daehne, Tracker added a note on the pad. Klaus Schmidt, radio operator. Loner. Sick when arrived, hospitalized. Later worked in stables.

He rhythmically tapped the pencil on the desk, then closed the notepad. Daehne's a tight ass. Angry. Maybe a little too proud. (And you know what they say about pride before...) "Hey, J. C., what's the name of the cook from the *Columbus*?"

"Gerhardt Müeller," Chávez answered, stepping into the office.

"What do you say we check out their mess?" Especially the knives, he thought.

"Done did it—first thing."

"We'll do it again. Another pair of eyes."

···

J. C. posted two men with guard dogs at each doorway to the room. Eleven o'clock—the small galley was crowded. Five stewards fighting for space. They all snapped to attention at the sight of the American officers. Only a slight, red-haired man kept working.

"Müeller?" snapped Tracker.

The chef answered in heavily-accented English, "One moment." He flipped an omelet in a frying pan, set the pan aside, wiped his hands. "For Captain. He eats alone. Ship's routine, like bells."

Tracker frowned. Damn annoying, those bells.

"We have our own watch. Good for morale," Müeller said, mispronouncing the last word as 'moral.'

"Do you remember who was on watch yesterday evening?"

"No, I busy with dinner."

Sounds of a scuffle outside the door. Aggressive growling. J.C. spun around, hand on his firearm. A tall, frightened steward hurriedly stepped inside, tripped, sending his tray of sandwiches across the floor. He scrambled to pick them up.

Müeller shouted, "We have nothing to waste. Be careful!" The small-boned chef shrugged, "Sorry. I learn hard way here, cook what you give us. My specialty, *mett*, minced raw pork and onions, I don't make anymore. Pork from your suppliers—not clean."

"You said 'raw' pork?" Tracker cringed.

"In homeland we raise few pigs at a time. Very clean pens. For *abend brot*, our evening bread, we make *mettwurst* with only freshly-butchered pork." Müeller told him what had happened the last time he had served it. Thirty crewmen sick. Two died. Poison.

"Food poisoning. Trichinosis?" said Tracker.

"*Ja.* They're buried in cemetery up on hill, far away from other sailors. Why? You think God would separate Germans from other nationalities? A dead man is a dead man." Emphasis on *man.*

"You feed everyone, officers and crew?"

"*Ja.* Two shifts, each meal."

"Klaus Schmidt. You knew him?"

"Klaus good friend. We went to gymnasium together. He lived in chateau at edge of village. I was once there, the dining room I remember had huge round table. I count chairs, thirty-two. His father was *von*, you know?"

Müeller said Klaus loved fine food and liquor. His father was rich. Most Germans faced years of depression, deprivation. The galley crew had stopped working. Sandwiches still on the floor.

"Why wasn't Klaus an officer with that background?"

"Klaus wanted to be radioman. Went to communication school. Wanted to hire on ship, travel the world." Klaus had gotten the first job he applied for, because of luck, or family influence, Müeller was never sure. The *Columbus* was a thirty-two-thousand-ton, 775-foot, fast and luxurious cruise ship catering exclusively to the rich.

Müeller bragged about the ship's elaborate library. Massive pillars, gigantic murals. Passengers dancing under enormous chandeliers in the double-deck ballroom. Three hundred at a seating in the *Speise Salle 1*ˢᵗ *Klasse*. Fed from his galley.

"His politics?" Tracker asked.

"Klaus much impressed with new government of Germany. He said it was only hope for German people."

"Sounds like the Nazi party line to me."

"No. He was nationalist. Refused to join Socialist Party, like we all. To call him Nazi would be big insult. I was friend, you know."

"Someone sure didn't like him. Must've had a mighty good reason to mutilate..."

A bell rang the half hour. "Sorry. Must finish captain's lunch. It is cold."

"Go ahead, but keep talking."

Müeller wedged himself behind the narrow work station, pulled a long icepick-like instrument from a case. The leather roll was open, black wood knife handles all facing Müeller. The chef loaded the skewer with link sausages, piercing each one vertically, then placed it on the hot grill.

Without looking up, he said to Tracker, "Gift from my Mother. Used her savings for my knives. The only thing I took when *Columbus* went down."

"Any missing?"

Müeller handed it to him. A thong dangled from the worn case. Tracker examined each knife. "Very sharp."

"Never out of my sight."

Tracker held up an eight-inch, slightly curved, slender blade.

"Boning knife. Beautiful, *ja*? With that I bone, skin delicate fish like trout—fast."

Tracker slid the knife firmly back in its slot, saying, "Maybe I'll do some fishing, bring my catch to you to fillet."

"I have time."

As if suddenly a part of the conversation, a steward chided the chef, "Don't be such pessimist. We're home by autumn, yes?"

Müeller shook his finger at the man. "By Christmas, maybe."

"*Ja*, Christmas, maybe," the young man said.

Müeller slid the sausages next to the omelet. "Every day our captain say we are seamen in transit. But we are distressed seamen with no transit."

Landlocked. No ship in sight. Unlike the captain, the pride in his voice had disappeared.

Tracker stepped into bright sunlight. Ahead of him by six paces, J. C. took the whistle from the chain around his neck, blew it shrilly. The dogs led the way. Two guards in the northeast tower, rifles ready, followed Tracker's every move. Time stopped in the camp, a vaporous mirage hovered between the barracks. Haloes shimmered around the tin roofs, coils of barbed wire, even the whitewashed rocks lining walkways. A barber held his scissors in midair over a POWs head. Machinists in the blacksmith shop stepped back from the anvil. Laundry hung limp on the lines.

The main gate opened. Tracker and J. C. sidestepped a row of wheelbarrows near the headquarters building. In a trench being dug for a new foundation, internees stood silently below them, shovels in hand, heads down.

J. C. blew the whistle again. A guard dog barked. The day resumed.

"Do they usually act this way?" Tracker asked.

"Daehne's hard on them, very strict, but I think they're all spooked, too, what with the murder." Tracker grunted. "Besides, you're new, and damned intimidating."

•••

Back at his desk, his eyes on the impeccable handwritten German script in Daehne's log, he thought of the Germans he had known during his youth in Kansas. Stalwart farmers. Strong-willed, hard workers. Disciplined, and damn proud of their heritage. Years later he had stood and stooped next to German workers in the beet fields of Colorado. One man in his early twenties, Hans Ritter, had escaped Germany as World War I threatened Europe. He came from an aristocratic family, but mentioned it only once. He taught himself English using a Bible with German on one page, English on the other.

The smell had bothered him the most. A putrid, stomach-turning stink hung over those Colorado beet fields. Rot. Toxic, sulfuric rot. Tracker and Hans slept head-to-toe in a shanty. They couldn't escape the smell. No money for soap. Hans told him the hardships would make them better men. They would get out of the sweatshops in the sun, have jobs and clean fingernails. They would never bow to the fat cats of the Great Western Sugar Company. Never be subservient or intimidated again.

J.C.'s knock on his door caught his attention. "Clara made some burritos. Want one?"

"Perfect. How is everyone? Clara, Linda? Haven't seen them since you moved up here." Tracker opened the waxed paper wrapped tortilla, took a huge bite.

"We finally found a little cabin near Ruidoso. Moved out of my uncle's place. Rustic, no phone, but it's on the river. Nice, cool. Trout, too." J.C. swallowed the last of his burrito, brushed off his shirt front, pulled out his comb. Cocked his head, checking his reflection in the glass window, swept his dark hair straight back.

Tracker watched, familiar with the younger Hispanic's fastidious and vain ways. Always pressed, polished. Good-looking, arched black eyebrows like all the Chávez men. Short, strong. Loads of natural savvy. A good mechanic. Figures out how things work. Close cut hair. Dark brown eyes. Muscular and quick. Not impetuous, except for falling in love with Clara and getting married in less than a month. Very protective of her and their two-year-old daughter.

Jimmy could also disappear. Before you know it, he's gone with no trace.

6

Two workmen shouted over the din of a buzz saw. Nothing new to add to his list. The only good news was Tracker could move out of his coffin-sized room into his own quarters by the end of the week. A roll of tar paper fell off the roof. A worker laughed as another cursed loudly in German. "That does it. J.C., give me the keys to the jeep."

He returned the salute of a canine patrolman, and thought for a minute the Austrian Shepherd was going to salute as well. He drove across the river, passed the marine hospital, the only semblance of civilization for miles in every direction. Must be the most remote hospital in America. He headed east, away from Fort Stanton. The rutted road curved its way up to another plateau and the cemetery. He parked, grabbed his crutch. Ducking under the chain, he came upon a massive ship's anchor at the foot of a twenty-foot-high white marble obelisk. Simple white crosses marked with tin plates radiated precisely. Mariners from around the world. Scandinavians, Japanese, Europeans, Americans.

Looking across the dramatic drop to the valley to the distant Capitán Mountains, he followed the green ribbon of cottonwood trees along the Rio Bonito. After his tenure on the border, the view before him was sweet comfort.

He knew the entire area had seen harsh times. People that managed to keep their land during the Depression could spit dust balls at the White House and FDR's so-called New Deal plan. Ranchers fed their stock anything that managed to grow. Tumbleweeds, Russian thistle. Cattle chewed cottonwoods. Aspens were scarred. What the weather didn't starve, the stock market plunge wiped out. The cattle market was, well, non-existent.

A large turkey vulture swooped low, squawking a hoarse cry. The iridescent black plumage flashed in his peripheral vision. He held his hand above his sunglasses to shield his eyes, slowly turning in a circle. 1.1 million acres of the Lincoln National Forest surrounded him.

How could he ever expect to find the scalp?

He didn't know how long he had been standing there when his gaze focused on two white crosses far apart from the rest in the northwest corner. The crosses identified the graves as Germans: Otto Steub and

Wilhelm Kasner. The two seamen who died of trichinosis. Now a third sailor on the way to join them.

■■■

Backtracking, Tracker noticed a vaguely familiar Chevy pickup behind the hospital. He parked the jeep at an angle in front of the truck. Reached down for his crutch. A large man appeared from behind, slammed the tailgate shut and stepped back. As tall as Tracker, but his legs were bowed, the build of a born horseman. A big guy, long-waisted, truncated neck. Pressed shirt, snap buttons. The man took off his Stetson, exposing a full head of white hair.

"You must be the new chief."

"Senior Patrol Inspector Dodds."

"Albert Grafton, from over in the Hondo Valley. I'm the rancher supplying the meat for your good folk and the hospital. I was just leavin' the paperwork."

"You made a delivery late yesterday to the camp?"

"Yep, usually try to make it on Thursdays."

"Notice anything unusual that evening?"

"Nothin'. Why?"

"There's been a death in the camp. You see or hear anything?"

"Someone killed?"

"A sailor died, one of the *Columbus* crew."

Grafton hooked his fat thumbs on his Levi pockets. "That bunch. Most locals like'em."

"The locals aren't anti-German?"

"Hell, no, before the damn Japs bombed Pearl Harbor, they let'em go into Carrizozo, Capitán. Funny, they called it 'shore leave.' Some of 'em came back delightfully inebriated. Sometimes they went clear over to Roswell. The store people were real appreciative—the Germans spent real money. We've lost all our young men 'round here to the draft. The café in Capitán is threatening to close. That money meant a lot to those folks."

Grafton had his eyes on Sierra Blanca. A dark anvil cloud was forming, accompanied by deep rumbling. "Storm's brewin'. Lord knows we need rain. It's so dry, the trees are bribing the dogs."

Tracker chuckled, then asked, "You always make the deliveries yourself?"

"Sometimes I have my foreman do it. No sweat for me, though. The

Germans do the unloading. They're industrious as hell, lots of skilled talent on that ship. Planted all those trees and shrubs you see out there. Built that swimming pool. Efficient, got it done. When I saw that, I had some of 'em fix up my bunkhouse with plumbing, do some work on my fence lines. Mind you, your men were on horseback, guardin'em. I paid eighty cents in scrip a day. Hey, now, got to be goin'—here comes the rain."

Tracker turned toward the hospital. Grafton revved his truck, calling out the window, "Sometime soon why don't you bring yourself and the ladies over to my place," he added, nodding toward the hospital. "That chief nurse is a real looker. I'll fix y'all dinner."

▪▪▪

A looker, thought Tracker, who had known many. Especially during his flat-broke days after having to drop out of Texas A & M. He went on the barnstorming circuit. Not a girl in every port, but every airport. At air shows, faking dogfights, competing in flashy aerobatics.

He had barnstormed from early spring until after harvest. Off season he did mail carrying and the occasional smuggling. It was addictive.

He saw himself walking away from the apron. A female figure would inevitably emerge from the crowd. He left his leggings and unlaced boots under many a bed. Always leaving in the dark, mentally telling himself he was too much a risk-taker to enter into a relationship with any decency. He felt like he used women as a refuge from hard times. And not proud of it, he thought as he negotiated the hospital stairs one at a time.

▪▪▪

Dr. Stillington was in an office no larger than a cubicle, hardly room for the desk and chair. The venetian blinds were closed, blocking the view of the old cavalry parade ground. A pile of newspapers were stacked in a corner. From where he stood, all Times—Picayune. Expensive to have papers mailed all the way from New Orleans. A photograph of an antebellum home hung on the wall above, impressive Doric columns supporting the tall portico.

"Doctor, you sounded intrigued. What've you got?"

"I don't know how much of this you will understand."

Tracker leaned heavily on his crutch. "Try me." He was tired, it was late. His leg was killing him. No place to sit down. A shooter. Straight from his spine to the heel of his foot.

The first time it had happened, he screamed, then fainted. The surgeon who had treated him had warned him of intermittent electric shooting pain. It wasn't an injury limited to the leg. There were big ramifications concerning his lower spine. The injury had been very severe. Debilitating. Why the hell had El Paso headquarters shipped him here? Compared with the 24/7 bustle of El Paso-Juárez, maybe they guessed that he would get plenty of time to rest. But, hell no. Constant construction. Constant additions to the internment population. Now he was getting Nazis. If only he could sit down. Just sit down and rest. Stillington hunched over his desk, studied a stack of papers. "First off..." he began, still not looking up. "When I palpated, that is, pushed on the abdomen, I could tell it was filled with fluid. I could even elicit a fluid wave. So, I needled it, and pure blood—not a hint of any clotted blood, as I told you, filled the syringe. Agent Dodds, are you listening?"

"Pure blood, not clotted blood. Do you have another chair? My leg..."

Stillington grumbled, stood up. "Take mine. I'll move right along." He moved over to the window, one hand on the sill, feet crossed.

For some reason, Tracker focused on the doctor's argyle socks. If he was going to faint, at least he was sitting.

Stillington continued, speaking without inflection or emotion. He had drained the abdominal cavity of the unclotted blood, once more emphasizing the term *unclotted.* When he opened the abdomen, the walls presented with pinpoint hemorrhages, or petechiae, as he called them. The liver revealed a sponge-like bruise where it had apparently been pressed against a rib. The kidneys appeared normal and the intestinal tract appeared normal as well. When he examined the exposed abdominal aorta—the giant artery situated just in front of the oval body portion of the spinal column—what on first impression seemed to be a rupture was, in fact, a tear at the level of the eleventh and twelfth vertebrae.

There was also a scratch and pit on the body of the twelfth vertebra. Looking at the abdominal skin once pulled back in place, he could visualize the path of the penetrating instrument. It had entered the abdomen just below the sternum or breast bone, as he explained to Tracker, then pierced soft tissue, including the lower edge of the liver, the mid-portion of the stomach, an edge of the pancreas, through the large aorta, finally stopping when it struck the boney vertebral body.

"That means whoever did this was going to be absolutely sure damage was done," Stillington concluded.

"Was the killer educated in medicine?"

"Interesting question. Could be...but anyone bent on killing could have done it. Remember, there was a horrible amount of damage to vital organs."

"You said you were puzzled over what you found. What exactly is puzzling you?"

"I believe I said I was intrigued, Mr. Dodds. His scalp was ravaged, virtually adzed from his cranium, yet the victim's body did nothing, not a single visible thing, to try and stop the bleeding. There was virtually no visible evidence of any clot formation in the aorta, or any of the invaded organs." Dr. Stillington repeated himself. "Absolutely no evidence of a clotting mechanism."

"Clotting mechanism. Exactly what do you mean?"

"Are you familiar with the fact that if you cut your finger, bleeding begins, and slowly it stops. There are numerous particles and chemicals in the bloodstream itself plus elements from bone marrow that all play a role in making the clot...the plug that stops the bleeding. It takes time for a lab to check each element in the plugging process to see if one or more are missing."

Stillington's watery blue eyes were magnified by his reading glasses. Tracker couldn't tell if the doctor's expression was one of sadness or detachment. He asked about the lab tests.

"Those..." he paused, took off his glasses, rubbing the bridge of his nose. "Blood samples, bone marrow. We will see..."

Tracker turned the wipers on to clean off the dirtball-spotted windshield. Grafton was partially right, the shower was more wind and dust than rain, but the river was up. Heavy rain somewhere high on the mountain. He backed down the street behind the hospital, swung north, out of the Fort. At the juncture with the main road, Pluck saw him first and bounded toward him. Tracker slowed to a stop, leaned out the open door to ruffle the dog's ears. Pluck's tail beat a steady rhythm against the door.

Kate joined them, saying with a laugh, "We got caught in the rain—all ten minutes of it. Not a good time for a walk—my hair is a wreck."

"Pluck seemed to like it," said Tracker. "Though he's a little smelly."

"Nice though, to have a shower this time of day."

"In New Mexico, it's nice to have rain anytime." Tracker swung his legs out of the Jeep, pulled himself to a standing position beside her. "J. C.

told me that you can recognize a native New Mexican by the fact they send their kids out into the rain. It's in case they move to another state, they'll know what rain is." She swept her damp hair back and smiled at him.

They both heard the music at the same time. Muted at first, rising both in volume and intensity as the sound of the trumpets reached them from across the river.

"It's the ship's orchestra," Kate said.

The prevailing breeze from the west, carrying the music to where they stood. After a moment, Tracker said, "I hate to admit this, but when I heard the ship had a band, I expected um-pah-pah or some bombastic Wagnerian stuff. But this is great."

"Billie Holiday," said Kate, arms across her chest, head cocked to one side. "Wonder if they realize it's about racial discrimination? They're very good—makes me feel sorry for the prisoners, especially the sailors from the *Columbus*."

"If I were in their place, I would sure feel bitter, bitter towards America, and their own government for starting the war. But that ship tried to run a blockade. Those men are enemy aliens."

"It's not fair, and you know it," Kate said, tightening her arms with a shiver. Though she had never experienced any of the elements of war, she had experienced being ostracized by someone. In her mind, it was the worst isolation a human could experience. Tracker watched her close her eyes, mutter something barely audible. At that moment he realized she was a vulnerable soul. And an enigma.

"No, it's not fair," said Tracker. "It's war."

Tracker drove slowly back to the compound, parked at the northeast baseline, snapped a salute to the guard in Tower #1.

It was downtime in the camp, but volunteer internees were clearing an area near the river for a soccer field. His predecessor had approved the project—anything to lessen pent-up tension. High on a scaffold in front of the nearest barracks, two prisoners were whitewashing the rough planks with calcimine. The doors and windows were wide open, the temperature hovered in the eighties. Just inside the door, Tracker could see two POWs leaning forward on their cots over a wooden crate, concentrating on a serious game of chess. In the distance, he heard music—the ship's orchestra was still practicing.

All deceivingly calm.

A quadrant of floodlights surrounding two auxiliary generators lit up near Columbus Hill. Even from where he stood he could hear both generators humming with high voltage electricity. He paused beside the tall radio antenna adjacent to headquarters, took a deep breath. The air was filled with the unmistakable smell of ozone; more rain on the way. In the distance, teams of dog handlers passed each other, tails wagged, then drooped.As he entered headquarters, he heard Mexican music playing on the radio. He recognized the call sign as XELO, the well-known "border blaster" in Ciudad Juárez. At 50,000 watts, it claimed to be heard as far away as New York City. Beaver turned it down, and asked if he wanted some cold fried chicken. Tracker ignored him, but stopped short of his office door. "Fried chicken?"

"Not exactly. Prairie chicken. With gravy. Shot and cleaned it myself."

Tracker's eyebrows went up a bit. "Believe I will."

"You won't regret it," Beaver said, removing a checkered flour sack from a platter. "Vinegar pie for dessert. I'm gonna evaporate some of that cloud of pessimism drownin' you. Here you go, sir. Chicken and biscuits and hot gravy."

Beaver took a seat opposite Tracker. "You go on and eat up. If you don't mind, I'm gonna talk." Tracker nodded, a piece of gravy-soaked bis-cuit already in his mouth.

"You know, I'm a crack shooter, never been moved up. I know my place—it is where I take my mind. New Mexico is free. Good people. I don't drink, don't get angry, love my cookin' 'cus it pleases people."

"That makes you the only happy soul in these parts," said Tracker.

A mariachi band was winding down on the station based out of Juárez. "Music okay with you, Agent Dodds?"

"I'm used to it. Probably the only signal you can get up here."

"Don't you love the preacher that comes on selling autographed pictures of Jesus Christ with eyes that glow in the dark?" Beaver chuckled. "Five dollars a pop. What a crock. What's your favorite song?"

"Can't think of one right off." Tracker hunched over the table, leaning on his elbows, put down his knife and fork.

"Oh, my poor soul. Nothing that gets your feet moving? Gets you in the mood?"

"No."

"You are one uptight hombre, Agent Dodds. Something deeper than your bum leg has been gnawing on you for a long time. You never laugh, much less smile. You can smile, can't you?" Beaver, eyes wide, added with exasperation, "Go for a ride. Breathe in this mountain air. Take some time for yourself. Get your blood pressure down."

"Appreciate the observation," said Tracker, wiping his mouth with the back of his hand. "Compliments to the chef. Where did you learn to cook like this?" A clean leg bone clattered on his tin plate.

Beaver laughed. "I was raised on corn dodgers, sorghum mo-lasses, bacon and cheese."

"You said your mother was Mexican."

"Sir, don't be hurtin' my feelings. I did have a father. From Joplin, Mossouri to El Paso, Texas. Came out West for the clean air, met my mother in Juárez. He didn't make it to age thirty, but he was a force of nature. Killed in World War I. I still have his Medal of Honor."

"Thank you for your father's service. So you grew up in El Paso?"

"Yes. Loved to hike in the desert. Cleaned by the sun."

"And wind."

"Yes, sir, what about your father?"

Beaver was quick to respond to Tracker's silence. "More pie, Agent Dodds?"

2

Despite Beaver's good cooking, a second night of restless sleep. More tired now than when he turned out the light. The room smelled dusty. The previous tenant left a soiled T-shirt now wrapped in a spider web in the corner. A half-empty box of cartridges sat next to it. A wooden crate held some empty bottles. He sat up. Slowly. With a thud, a book dropped to the floor.

A reader since he could ever remember. Like a craving, he saw himself wanting a book back in Colorado. Still just really a kid, and on his own at sixteen, he took the only job available. Whacking beet tops with a machete in blasting heat. One afternoon, dead tired, and with nowhere to go, Tracker had found himself on the Post Office steps in Greeley. Other poor kids were in line, waiting for the canvas sides of the book-wagon to go up.

Three books at a time. Tracker was saved. Dostoyevsky. Tolstoy. Dumas. Dickens and Doyle. H. G. Wells, especially the serials he wrote for *Cosmopolitan.* And anything on aviation. Aeronautical Society bulletins. *Fly* magazine, and the *Aerial Reporter.*

But the first fall brought bad news. Union County couldn't afford a teacher or a wagon driver. At age seventeen, he volunteered to do both in exchange for a cot in the schoolhouse. That job lasted until spring.

Aching to learn how to fly, he hitchhiked to Denver. Double shifts at the Brown Palace. Bellman during the day. Bouncer at the Ship's Tavern at night. A wise bartender who hailed from Texas told him about the cadet corps at Texas A & M. Tracker aced the admission exams, got a scholarship.

Enough memories.

He limped to the dresser, the single piece of furniture in the room other than the cot. The water pitcher was empty. "Beaver! Water, damnit!"

"Sorry, sir. I thought Maxwell had..." Beaver put the enameled tin pitcher on the dresser and backed away, hands crossed behind his back.

"No excuses. I know it's a small thing, but damn..."

"Won't happen again, sir. I promise. Can I get you anything else? Your crutch?"

"Pl Beaver, did I detect you feeling sorry for this gimp-legged old fart? Do you think that headquarters put this sorry soul up here to run herd on five-hundred goddamned foreigners if I wasn't up to it?"

Dressed only in his olive drab boxer shorts, Tracker caught his own reflection in the mirror, as well as the furrowed brow of the wizened black patrolman. Beaver was looking at his withered leg, which put Tracker's temper on boil.

"I used to be a pilot," Tracker began in a low roar. "A damn good one, too." After his tour with the border patrol, he planned to enlist. Especially when he heard about the Doolittle raid—he wanted so damn bad to join the Air Corp right then.

"After breakfast," Tracker said tiredly, "Saddle up the best horse we've got."

"Yes, sir!"

Tracker poured water into the basin and leaned on the dresser. His mother had told him that as a hungry infant, he could really tie on a full-blown tantrum. A waste of energy, she always said. He adjusted his tie, jerking the knot tight.

The eggs over easy were perfect, which made Tracker feel like a grouchy shit. He apologized to Beaver, adding that he was going to ride the camp perimeter. Beaver started to offer to go with him, but thought better of it. Tracker positioned his hat, stepped into rain-chilled air. The Appaloosa sidestepped nervously as he approached. He checked the cinch, propped his crutch against the hitching post, and set his left foot in the stirrup. Gritting his teeth, he swung his bad leg over the saddle and settled into the seat. Not as bad as he expected.

Beaver stepped out on to the porch, snapped a salute. "Well done, sir."

Tracker grunted. The Appaloosa was skittish. "Easy there, boy. Easy."

"He's J.C.'s favorite mount. The best we got. Treats him like he belongs to him."

"We'll see about that. Remind him that I outrank him."

Beaver smiled. "Yes, sir."

Following the barbed wire-topped fence, he headed up the hill toward the mountain. He was tracking the point of emergence of the sun in the east. Long cast shadows fooled his mind. He turned his back to the emerging light. The shadow of man and horse stretched more than double their combined height. Moisture clung to the piñon and juniper, highlighting each outline as the sun breeched the horizon.

Like Beaver said, thin mountain air, turquoise sky. Soft breeze from the east. Chamisa, Indian paintbrush, white jimson flowers. Far from the international border where the predominant smells were exhaust fumes, Chevron and Texaco refinery's sulphur dioxide emissions, dust and hot asphalt.

He realized his blood pressure was back to normal. Beaver's advice was working.

"God almighty!" he yelled, as the Appaloosa suddenly shied, veering straight into a juniper tree, just missing the lurch of another horse lunging over the side of the steep arroyo. The black and white dog charged up the incline to him.

"Hey, Pluck," called Tracker, brushing needles from his shoulder and neck.

"Didn't hear you coming—I'm sorry," said Kate.

"You ride up here every day?" Tracker asked, pulling his horse alongside her buckskin. The Appaloosa whinnied lowly, and the two horses began the ritual of swatting tails. Sunlight touched her face.

"When I can, depends on my shift." She squinted in the growing sunlight and reached in her shirt pocket for sunglasses.

Surprised at the soft timbre of her voice, he reminded himself not to say anything the slightest bit provocative. That's why he flinched as she placed two fingers in her mouth, whistled loudly for Pluck. Without another word, she trotted away.

She stopped at the top of the ridge and looked back at him. He held his hat at his side, the sunlight glinted off his greying hair. It appeared to have a slight reddish tinge she hadn't noticed before. The shadows on his face strengthened his weathered features. A memorable face, she thought, as she called to him, "Busy tonight?"

Caught off guard again, he said, "No...no, nothing on."

"Dinner at Albert Grafton's?"

"He didn't ask me."

"I have."

"I'll pick you up?"

"At five. It's about an hour's drive to his ranch."

...

"I'll drive," Kate said.

"No," Tracker snapped. So we begin the evening, he mused.

"But your leg...where's your crutch?"

"I don't need the crutch and my driving has nothing to do with my leg. Besides, I have a cane. Would you please get in?"

"Are you always so obdurate?" asked Kate. Tracker laughed. "I've always wanted to use that word."

"Ladies, please." He opened the door. He had placed a wood plank over the cargo box, tossed a tattered pillow on top. Underneath, an organized stack of steel cable, ropes. Winch with a heavy duty snatch block and clevis D-shackle. Gloves. Tow straps. Shovel. Flashlight. Binoculars. Hand cuffs. Truncheon. Pick axe. Canteen, Cartridge shells next to a carefully wrapped shotgun.

Izzie deferred to Kate and slipped into the back. Tracker noticed his shirt cuffs were dirty, quickly rolled up his sleeves.

"You combed your hair," said Kate.

He shifted into gear, tires crunched on the gravel driveway. "I like it."

Tracker saluted to the guard at the hospital checkpoint. "I'm not accustomed to escorting ladies. Especially in civilian clothes." He wore a black vest over a once-white shirt. Pearl snaps on the pockets. His "good" Tony Lama boots. Actually a pair that were too tight for Chief Vonshooven. He bought them for the little cash he had in his pocket at the time. Clean Levi's.

The route to the Grafton ranch was narrow, winding, and rutted. The sound of the engine prevented much chatter. Both girls were holding on to whatever they could. Kate swept her short hair back, smiled at Tracker. She couldn't see his expression behind his dark glasses, but just having a man next to her felt damn good.

Though the juniper-covered hills were already in deep shadows, the tips of the distant Capitán Mountains were still in full sunlight. As the sun dropped behind Sierra Blanca the reflected rays of light glazed the easternmost Capitáns a deep rose. The road improved slightly when they turned left onto Highway 70 just after Glencoe. A drop in altitude. The valley spread before them, surprisingly green considering the drought. Horses grazed in the shadows of poplar-lined ranch roads.

On the outskirts of San Patricio they passed the White Cat Bar, Kate spoke up. "Turn at that gate up ahead. Nine miles to the ranch. Izzie, you okay back there?"

Tracker watched her in the rearview mirror. Face like a blank canvas, except for gold flecks in her dark brown eyes. Hair parted down the center. Short hair in front, like a bob. But her hair in back was long, coiled on each side. Coils shaped like squash blossoms. A special design, that of an unmarried Hopi girl. She wore a finely woven blanket over one shoulder, which nearly hid her necklace, three strands of turquoise nuggets. A black narrow-pleated broom skirt. Wine red blouse, silver buttons to the top. A silver concho belt.

The cattle guard groaned as they crossed it. The jeep dropped into a deep rut, rudely tossing all of them. "Whoa, steady there, girl." He glanced in the rearview mirror. "Izzie, you still okay?"

Izzie said something in Hopi, then readjusted the thin blanket over her shoulders. For a second, Tracker thought he saw two black crosses painted on her right upper arm. Tattoos?

"You could have taken that a little slower," Kate said. She shot him a look. Almost a curious smile. In contrast to Izzie, Kate wore a fitted white blouse, two contoured darts front and back, and tan gabardine slacks. The wide collar lapels lay back casually, and Tracker couldn't help but notice the top two buttons weren't fastened.

The road smoothed, he sped up. Over the sound of the engine down-shifting, he said, "I'm guessing you're not from here."

"Wyoming. Laramie. As the crow flies, six hundred or so miles from here."

"And your folks? Are they still there?"

"My father's a lawyer." Kate looked straight ahead. "Was a lawyer. He died, heart attack."

"I'm sorry."

"I like to think he's free now." She clenched her fingers tightly to-gether on her lap, then released them. "We were very close. Besides his practice, he was into all kinds of things—a real entrepreneur. I grew up on a mink farm."

"Mink farm?"

"He owned one in Canada. He took me up there with him a lot, just the two of us. Smuggled hooch, too."

"Smuggler, eh?"

She laughed, a sparkling, energetic laugh. A first. "He gave me a car when I was only fourteen, a yellow Chrysler roadster with a rumble seat. It made me feel so grown up, driving through the snow, my daddy puffing away on his pipe. We were all bundled up in mink coats—I had four of them, all different lengths."

"You needed all four, I'm sure."

"Yes," she said, ignoring his sarcasm. The image of her mother flashed in her mind. A thin, delicate woman dressed in black, seated in her wheelchair, Elizabeth MacAllan, also an attorney. She loved nothing more than to win a case, whether her client was innocent or guilty. But when it came to her daughter, Kate was always guilty. Kate's obvious love for her father hadn't made things easier.

Kate would have been the second female law student accepted at the University of Wyoming, but she had no regrets in turning it down. When she told her mother she wanted to be a nurse, her mother had gone into a rage, suddenly standing up from her wheelchair. With a move she would never ever forget, the most proper Mrs. MacAllan took several quick steps toward her and slapped her face hard. Kate was too shocked to cry. In a commanding, tortured voice, Kate had screamed, "Mother, I hate you! I hate you!"

With the quiet help of her father, without regrets, she moved to Denver, went to nursing school. Though he visited when he could, her mother never came, never wrote, never mentioned her name again.

The Jeep passed over another cattle guard marking the entrance to the Grafton ranch headquarters. The buzz of the tires on the iron grate helped to jar Kate's bad memories. They passed between two tall adobe pillars supporting a heavy, round *viga* and a sign: *El Rancho Venado*.

"I like it," Tracker commented. "The ranch of the deer."

"You speak Spanish?"

"Surprised? Actually, all us red-blooded border guys have to, a requirement for the job."

Ahead, poplar trees lined both sides of a dirt road leading to a sprawling ranch house. Slowing to cross a bridge over the almost-dry Hondo River, he dodged cattle, cow pies all the way down the dusty driveway.

He parked in front of a pair of weathered doors recessed into a thick adobe wall. One tall panel opened and a tall, slender young man with shoulder-length black hair stepped forward.

"Paul, bring'em in. Time's a'wasting," called Grafton, appearing behind his foreman. Grafton was wearing a cream-colored straw hat, spotless white shirt, tan slacks, large turquoise- encrusted belt buckle.

"Dear ladies, I am honored. Welcome to you, son, a pleasure. This is my main man, Paul Chino—he's Apache, from Mescalero. Couldn't run the place without him. Say what, Paul, how 'bout opening the bar? Rev up our appetites before we load up that table."

"Right away, Mr. Grafton," Paul answered in a quiet voice.

"The ladies have heard this before. But for you, son," he said, focusing on Tracker. "You might be interested to know, the entrance in the perimeter wall wasn't always there. Used to be, to get to the house, whoever was on guard would lower a ladder from the inside. You'd climb over the wall into the *zaguan*, the entry court, and a guard would pull the ladder up after you. That wall was all that protected you from marauding Apaches. They'd just as soon kill everyone, burn the house down." Grafton wrapped his arm around Izzie's shoulders, saying, "My dear, no offense meant, but back in those days the Apaches were vicious."

"None taken, Mr. Grafton. I'm Hopi," Izzie reminded.

8

Grafton led the way into the living room. Tracker hesitated at the double doors. By the look of things, the rancher had done pretty well in life.

It was a room for men, with museum-quality art. A large oil of a buffalo hunter by Tom Lea. Edgar Curtis platinum photographs. Mantel lined with San Ildefonso pottery. Two Grey Hills rug. Germantown Dazzler blanket on the wall. Leather cushions softened by many a cowhand's butts.

An Acoma basket in need of repair rested on top of the Steinway. Izzie ran her fingers along the damaged edge at the top of the basket. "Mr. Grafton, where did you find this?"

"I was lucky enough to witness a child-naming ceremony. Unforgettable. At sunrise the medicine man took this basket filled with prayer sticks, lifted it way up, praying to the sun, then threw the basket over the edge of the cliff. He picked up the baby and stretched out his arms—damned near scared me to death, I thought he was going to throw the baby over, too. Sunlight hit the baby. Then he sucked in all the air he could, and blew the air out, saying the kid's name."

"He was giving the child the breath of life," said Izzie.

"Right," Grafton said. "Once that ceremony was all over, I scrambled down the canyon and picked up the basket."

"What are these?" Tracker asked.

Izzie spoke up again, "*Páhos. Kwávahos.* Something Mr. Grafton shouldn't have."

"Right you are, little lady, but I think they're interesting. Figured no one, not even the gods would care or take notice if I had snatched two of them prayer sticks." He held them out.

Seven to eight inches long. Sharp points. Three golden eagle feathers bound at the bevel.

"Kind of vicious things when you think about it," Tracker said, replacing the prayer sticks in the basket.

"I hold them in reverence," said Grafton. "These people were here a long time before us white men. They're in tune with nature. I respect them for that for sure."

In a more conversational tone, he asked, "What do you think of the place? Anything nice you see here, my late wife gave me. She made sure everyone would feel like they could walk in here with their boots on." He placed an arm on Tracker's shoulder. "Come on out back. Got to see what Paul has been making up for y'all."

Grafton headed through a door to his office, then the *cantina*, according to an old U. S. Cavalry Post Exchange sign above the door. When he noticed Tracker looking up at it, he said, "Got that from Fort Stanton. They left it there when the last garrison left in eighteen ninety-six."

"Why did the soldiers leave?" Tracker asked.

"Higher-ups decided the troops at Fort Stanton weren't needed anymore to provide protection from the Apaches." He explained between 1880 and 1890 how they had gained control of both the Warm Springs and Mescalero Apaches. Also, they had taken down their chiefs, Victorio, Nana, and Geronimo. "And that's your local history lecture for today."

The string of rooms were accessed room-to-room or from the patio doors along a covered porch. A massive elderly cottonwood shaded the patio.

Tracker stepped aside allowing the women to pass, his focus on the bookshelves. History. Medical and chemistry textbooks. On the lower shelf, twenty-four volumes of law books. A well-read host. Tracker swiveled around, thinking he heard Dr. Stillington's voice.

"I thought you were on a house call," said Kate, from the cantina doorway. "I didn't see your car."

The doctor was looking very genteel, very Big Easy. He wore a starched white shirt, floral-motif tie, but instead of his usual dark brown suit, he was wearing his summer fabric of choice, a light blue and white seersucker suit. He had once told Kate he had worn it every Sunday for brunch with his wife at Brennan's in New Orleans.

"I decided to come early," said Stillington. "I was worried about the weather. Did you all see those clouds over the mountain?"

"I did," said Tracker. "Where I came from that anvil-like formation meant tough weather's on the way, like a tornado."

"No tornadoes around here, son," Grafton commented as he handed Tracker and the doctor each margaritas. "Glad you made it, Doc. A toast to the great social lubricant from Mexico. Sure lucky we can still get *Jose Cuervo* in Juárez. Limes from my greenhouse. Paul's quite a gardener. Not too tart, is it?"

Stillington took a sip. Licked the salt from his lips. "*Perfecto*. The perfect margarita. What's the sweet?"

"Triple Sec. I have hoarded this baby for years."

"Bless you, sir."

"Thank you, Andrew. Like I said, no tornadoes, but sometimes you'd think you were in one by the force of those outfall winds. In our monsoon season, we get gushers, the kinda downpour that dumps maybe two, three inches in twenty minutes. You right quick discover what happens in those arroyos. Roarin' brown water carrying everything in its path, dead or alive."

Thunder rolled. Closer and closer. "Doctor, if you were so worried about the weather..." Tracker began to ask.

"Car trouble. Engine sounds terrible. Luckily, I made it here, thank God. Paul's the best mechanic around here. He's working on it in the barn. Something about a vapor lock."

"Come on, Tracker," said Grafton. "I'll show you how we cook around here. Grab that blue pitcher, will'ya? Hey, Paul, whip up another batch a'margaritas for doc and the ladies."

"It's ready, sir."

They stepped out onto the patio, walked to a four-by-five-foot rock-clad grill under the cottonwood. Pulling on a rope threaded through a block and pulley, Grafton heaved the blackened lid back open, exposing a whole side of beef on the grill. Cheeks flushed, perspiration on his forehead. He asked Tracker to refill his glass.

He wiped his eyes and brow with a handkerchief. "Ah, that's fine, son. Mercy, Lord knows we need rain bad. You know, this year I'm runnin' about two hundred head of cattle and more than two hundred and fifty lambing ewes. That livestock's competin' with the mule deer and prong-horns, gonna be forced to eat broom snakeweed and even locoweed soon just to stay alive."

A low-pitched roll of thunder reverberated directly above them. Both men glanced at the clouds, took a swallow. Through an arched gate, Tracker could see a rusty windmill about one hundred feet away. Blades were spinning at extreme velocity. Paul stood at the base, a look of concern on his face. When he turned back toward the house, Tracker looked away.

"Changing the subject. Remember me telling you one of the German prisoners had died?" Tracker said.

"Yes, one of the men from the ship."

"He was scalped."

Grafton put down the tongs. "You thinkin' an Indian did it?"

"We're investigating. It always boils down to motive. You seem to have a great deal of..."

"Sympathy for the Indians?" Grafton interrupted.

"Not sympathy, more like interest."

Grafton chuckled. "Yes, sir. I'm pretty well-read on the subject. My hobby, you might even say."

"Do you know anything about the ritual, the custom of scalping the enemy? Is it a battle trophy? An insult? Revenge?"

"Scalping goes way back." Grafton settled himself against the edge of the stone pit. The stemmed margarita glass teetered on the uneven surface. "Like the Scythians, for example." Tracker raised his eyebrows. "I know my history, son. The Visigoths did it, too."

"You mean the Germans?" Tracker swallowed the last of his drink. Most likely it was psychological, but he suddenly felt uneasy.

"Yes, they followed their code. Even the Anglo-Saxons took scalps, right up to the tenth century."

"What about the Native Americans?"

"Pour us another round. I love this stuff. Only make it for my honored guests." Grafton thrust his glass to Tracker. "You mean Indians in general, the Pueblos, or say, specifically the Hopis?"

"The Pueblos...and the Apaches, all of them," Tracker replied, trying to generalize, and not miss his glass as he poured.

"It's a fact, they all did it, one way or another. Sometimes they scalped them while the enemy was still alive. I believe they quit doing the ritual thing about nineteen-o-eight."

"Know anything about the technique—how you'd scalp someone?" The fire was hot, he was perspiring and knew the rancher could see rings of sweat on his shirt.

Grafton leaned close to him, his breath a mix of citrus and quality tequila. "Of course I do." In uncomfortably graphic steps he explained that you put your foot between the shoulder blades and the back of the neck, grab the hair on the crown of the head in one hand. Take a knife, cut through the skin to the skull and whack off a hunk of scalp.

"How big?"

He shrugged. "Size of your hand. They were pretty damned dexterous. I've read that some even used their teeth. Could tear off the whole hairy scalp in an instant."

Not quite the way Dr. Stillington said, but probably more accurate, Tracker figured. "I suspect there's a lot of bleeding?"

"Guess so. Scalp wounds tend to bleed a lot."

"Where do you think I could most likely find the scalp?"

"You won't."

"I won't?"

"The Apaches, like the Navajos, got rid of it right away, or right after they did the scalp dance."

"What about the Pueblo Indians, are they different?"

"Actually, I don't know much about the Hopi. Those people don't talk about it. Or anything else. They're real private people." Grafton watched Tracker, who obviously wanted more. More margaritas and more juice on Indian rituals. Both right up his alley.

He continued with stories about the Santa Domingo tribe. While they shared the same language, Keresan, the ceremonial rites were pretty different. He told Tracker when a Santa Domingan took a scalp, he would be called *O·pi*. The tribal trophies were kept by the *cacique*—the medicine man—in flour sacks in a cell below his living quarters. This room had no outside entrance. Every Sunday the scalps were washed and laid on blankets to dry. They kept the scalps softened by chewing on them.

Both men took a drink after that comment.

Grafton went on saying that on the twenty-fourth of June, San Juan Day, they were washed again, and before dawn, all men of the pueblo bathed in the river. After the scalps had been washed, the water was strained through cloths and medicine added to it. All the men would go to the scalp house where they received a drink of the liquid.

Throughout Grafton's recital, his tone of voice was void of emotion. Tracker also noticed the West-Texas accent was gone; Grafton even sounded professorial. "Have you always been a rancher?"

"Nope. I was trained as a lawyer—University of Chicago—worked for a time in Washington. Came out here, took one look at the sky, and never went east again. I best be takin' care of business here. Finish things up. Hand me that mop."

Grafton brushed a glaze on the meat, saying it was mostly vinegar and honey. "No sugar to be had with all the shortages. Townspeople bitchin' and moaning, but I'm accustomed to copin'."

The accent was back.

Grafton took another sip, saying, "I was just a baby when they sent me to France in World War I. While I was overseas, knee-deep in blood and mud, my daddy passed away. He left me a sizeable amount of money. I used it to buy land out here."During the Depression, Tracker thought. At rock-bottom prices.

As if reading his mind, Grafton said, "Want to know my secret? I steered clear of banks. Watched good places get foreclosed, tearing families to pieces. I got on famously with the homesteaders. I like to watch'em work their land. I have *educated* a whole lot of settlers. I let'em haul water from the *Rancho Venado* wells, even when I sometimes didn't have enough for myself. I encouraged'em to bring their kids to my private school house. Even when we butcher, I send'em beef. I help out when I can. But I know that no matter how much land the government gives'em, they can't make a living. Homesteaders got five years to complete a Final Proof Form. If they can't do that, they can't get a patent certificate. Without that certificate, you can't record your deed with the county registrar of deeds.

"See, Tracker, none of'em had the money to be real ranchers. When they couldn't prove up, they were willing to sell. I was their friend. The homesteaders always offered their property to me first."

Another roll of thunder echoed repeatedly around them, a cool breeze struck the treetops, rattling the cottonwood leaves. Cotton wisps drifted around them like butterflies. Tracker didn't notice. It was obvious. This man had been purposely setting up the homesteaders so he could expand his empire.

"Glad I put the meat on when I did. Not ready any too soon." He handed Tracker a pair of leather gloves, then pulled on a pair himself. "You pull on that chain, I'll pull on this one." Tracker dropped his cane, braced himself on his good leg.

The enormous hunk of beef rose slowly from the grill. Grafton slid a heavy board under the edge of the meat and wrestled the beef onto it. He tore off a bite and sampled it. "Well, butter my butt and call me a biscuit. Damn good. Let's get this into the kitchen."

Grafton didn't mention shattered families again.

Platters soon appeared. Earthenware pots of hot and cold dishes.

Pitchers of beer. Talavera plates. Cobalt blue hand blown glasses. Colorful napkins.

"Round up everyone, Tracker, dinner is served, *frontera* style" said Grafton. "Who in this illustrious bunch will say grace?"

Kate's hand went up, bringing looks of doubt from everyone. "I'm serious." She bowed her head, both hands reaching out to each side. Hands held all around. "Bless these sinners as they eat their dinners."

Snorts of laughter, chuckles followed, then the eating began.

Besides the beef, chile-hot-as-hell, frijoles, corn, squash, cucumbers, tomatoes, and fry bread. Paul brought in two more pitchers of cold beer and set them at either end of the dining table.

"Just what I need," Kate said. "My lips are burning up. God, Izzie, how can you eat all those *jalapeños*?"

Izzie winked over the top of her beer glass.

"Where did you get this beer? Tastes a lot like the German beer I grew up with back in Kansas," Tracker commented. "Dark lager—our neighbors were German immigrants."

"I got it from a Dutchman down in La Luz. He makes it with honey that he gets from old man Clay in Mesilla. We help each other out to get by. You said you're a Kansas boy, a Jayhawker," said Grafton.

"That I am."

"Some real good cattle country up that way. You miss it?"

"Honestly, I don't remember much. I was pretty young when I moved away."

Truth be that when he left Kansas, he blindly headed west. Some kind of vague and dumb notion of becoming a 'gentleman of the road'—a hobo. He had hopped a hotshot train outside of Newton, Kansas. Met a guy who said a new beet factory had opened in Longmont, Colorado. They were looking for men to work the fields and the refinery.

He had no idea the job would stink so bad.

Kate wondered why Tracker clammed up, but locked the question away to ask him later. He seemed uneasy. She changed the subject.

"Hey, Doc. How's that golf course plan of yours going? Any luck?"

Stillington was nearly a scratch golfer, but he hadn't played on a professionally-ranked course since his days in New Orleans. Sundays meant Bloody Marys on the first tee. Beer on the back nine. A boozy lunch and club sandwiches with his father-in-law and rich friends back at the Tack Room.

Stillington tossed that memory in the trash bin where it belonged, and said, "Perfect location in the meadow below the cemetery. I've designed a nine-hole course. Complete with rye grass for the greens. Tricky sand traps. On one of the tees, you can't see to the green." Stillington chuckled. "I'm about to send in my petition. The only thing that might swing it—no pun intended—is that we could use the Germans for labor. Whatever pay is fair. But you know the PHS."

"I would love it, Doctor. My father taught me to play. Can I see the plan?" asked Kate.

"Certainly, my dear." Stillington watched her glance at Tracker. Caught a flash of a smile.

Looking around the table, Grafton asked, "Everyone had enough? Plenty more."

"No, thank you, Albert," Stillington said. "Kate, are you up to it?"

Kate pushed back from the table, pulled out a cigarette. After Stillington lit it, she exhaled, saying, "You bet." Back in the living room, she handed her cigarette to Izzie, sat down at the piano bench and began playing.

Tracker recognized it. "Bessie Smith, *A Good Man is Hard to Find.*"

Kate smiled back. "Ain't that the truth?"

She was good at playing the blues: another side exposed of this complicated woman, and he said so. "Where did you learn to play?"

"Here and there," she replied, never looking up. "I love the blues, fits my moods." She smoothly shifted from a minor 3rd to a major 3rd.

"You're very good," said Tracker.

"I had a very good teacher," Kate replied.

She remembered the soft-spoken pianist's sincere look of concern. Miss Baker. Worried about the eight-year-old's chapped hands, scuffed knees, rough and dirty elbows. She didn't say much to Kate, just said she would soak her small hands in wet oatmeal. The potion would help sluff off the scaled skin. Miss Baker massaged her hands with lanoline to make her hands soft and pretty.

At the time, Kate was flattered that Miss Baker would spend time making her feel pretty. Not a sentiment she heard or experienced at home. But when her mother found out through the grapevine that Kate had help in grooming from a lowly piano teacher (she called her an ugly spinster) Mrs. MacAllan burst into rage.

In a whirl of screams and shock, Kate suddenly found herself hanging from a hook in the dark garage. It was still an open wound in her mind. A maid had informed her father, who had been out of town. He gently lifted her down, murmuring softly, caressing her small head, wiping her tears. And ignoring her wet skirt and the puddle beneath it. From then on, whenever Mr. MacAllan left on business, Kate went with him.

To spite her mother, Kate became an accomplished pianist. Returning to the present, Kate concluded the piece with a rush.

Tracker refused another beer, as did Izzie. He had watched her body language, which was next to nil. She had said virtually nothing the entire evening, and now stood silently behind Kate, drawing on the cigarette.

Tracker took inventory. The tequila and big meal had taken its toll. Dr. Stillington - asleep. Grafton - head down as well. Paul had disappeared. Suddenly the first wave of pelting rain and hail struck the tin roof. Kate's fingers paused above the keys. The din evolved into a cacophony of pounding rain, hail, thunder and screaming wind.

Suddenly awake, Grafton said, "We got ourselves a gully washer." The electricity went out.

9

Stillington declined the offer of a ride back to the hospital, adding, "Albert's offered one of his guestrooms. I'll drive back as soon as Paul figures out the problem with that damnable engine. Tomorrow's Sunday, who's on duty?"

"Izzie's on at midnight. I take over at seven."

"Keep a close watch on Philip Anderson—a critical time right now," said Stillington, handing his umbrella to Kate. "Tracker, be careful."

The poplars bent in the wind. Sturdy piñons and junipers were pummeled. Wild grasses flattened. The jeep slipped, caught, gained traction. It was slow-going. Clay soil sucked, small arroyos frothed, trees split, destroyed. They chugged along, all three focused on the road. Multiple lightning bolts cracked, flashed. They were climbing, gaining in elevation as they left the Hondo Valley. If anything, the storm was more violent, developing a mean streak. A jagged bolt of lightning ripped through the darkness to the earth. The entire landscape was momentarily lit bright with neon-blue explosions.

They were in the village of Lincoln, right by the courthouse. Across the street was *La Paloma*, the local saloon. A tall man holding a lantern stood at the screen door. The only spot of light in the entire village. Hand-painted signs in the window advertising COLD BEER & CURIOS looked out of place.

The rain drummed on the canvas roof. Wipers fought to keep up with the downpour. Lightning cracked feet away. A bolt closer to white than yellow, loaded with electricity, struck, then pulsed back into the blackness. The village disappeared behind them.

Tracker hunched his shoulders. A prickly sensation ran up the back of his neck. He tried to count the time between thunder and lightning, but the strikes were too close together. Water gushed, gouging the rocky soil, eroding the narrow track. The jeep dropped. Reverse/forward. Reverse/forward/groan. Spin/spin/caught. Tracker swerved to avoid a shower of rock.

Fishtailed. A limb slapped the roof. He couldn't see in front of the hood. Very slow, he crept forward. Like threading sand through an hour glass, they finally made it to the juncture leading up the valley to Fort

Stanton. Turned left. Headlights bouncing. Water frothed down the hills to the right. They were nearing the river, Tracker slowed, stopped. In the glow of the headlights he spotted a sea of black water. Complete darkness in the direction of the camp.

"My God," said Kate. "The Rio Bonito is over its banks."

"Way over," said Tracker. "We'd better wait'til it slows down before I try to get you over to the hospital. Power is out."

"I've got to get to the emergency generator. The patients—you heard Dr. Stillington," said Kate.

"We don't have a choice."

An hour passed, the rain never let up. Tracker tried to turn the engine. Only a shrill grinding and a thud. "Flooded. We'll have to walk to the camp. Izzie, there's a flashlight back there somewhere with my gear. Kate, give me that umbrella, stay close to me."

"Your cane," said Kate.

"I'm fine."

Stepping into the darkness, Tracker clutched an arm of each girl, sheltering them under the red and white-striped umbrella. Kate's soaked blouse clung to her like another layer of skin. Her nipples hardened in the cold. He noticed.

A voice yelled out from the black void. "That you, Mr. T?"

"Over here," Tracker called.

"Where the hell have you been?" J. C. stumbled through the mud, trying to avoid branches, boulders. Water poured off his hat, dripping on to his yellow slicker.

"Grafton's place, the storm held us up."

"The fence is gone. Washed downriver. Four men escaped."

"Shit!" snapped Tracker, figuring his murderer was probably one of them. He handed the umbrella to J. C., saying, "Get the girls to the kitchen, tell Beaver to take care of them."

"Beaver's out working on the fence. Should I notify the sheriff? The POWs are off federal..." Wind gusted, ripping, inverting the umbrella. J.C. jerked off his slicker, draped it over the women.

"I told you what to do, get them inside." Tracker limped toward the edge of the roaring river, bending forward, hand on his hat. In a flash of lightning, he saw a dead cow float by, eyes wide open. Carefully, he edged his way along the narrow ridge of high ground. Smell of flint. Granite against granite. Color gone, achromatic, no hue, no depth.

Ahead he spotted Beaver standing near the edge of the swirling, violent water, battling to drive a post into the ground. An odd rushing sound suddenly filled the air; moments later a rogue surge of water poured over the temporary bank, catching Beaver off balance. Tracker watched in horror as the man slid helplessly into the water. Beaver was caught in the undertow, slammed against boulders, trees. His arms reached up. Huge boulders from high above slammed his skull. His body flipped upside down, head submerged.

Tracker instinctively jumped back to avoid the wave, at the same time grabbing for a large branch lodged against a piñon tree. He slapped it down on the water in front of him, yelling for Beaver to grab for it. Beaver's body, thrashing in the mud-filled rampage, rushed past the life-saving branch.

Tracker ran down the bank, losing his foothold, dropping the flashlight, sliding as he tried to catch up with Beaver. He reached out in the darkness, grabbing in vain for support, a lifeline, anything.

Nothing. His bad leg buckled as he stumbled forward. He felt the slap of the frigid water. Involuntarily, he cried out in shock. He was sucked under, his body spinning in a vortex of mud, water and rock. His arms flung out in an attempt to swim, but he was twisting wildly in circles. Spinning to the surface, he gasped for air, desperately trying to get his bearings. An uprooted tree stump hit him from behind, its torn roots wrapping around his torso, gouging his skin. Driven by helpless panic, he kicked, wildly clawed for the bank. His eyes filled with silt, he wasn't sure if he was on the bottom being pummeled by the rocky bed or slamming against the bank. Rushing waves crashed over his body, darkness engulfed him.

He choked. Spit out gravel, grit. He searched for some source of stability. Clenched his teeth. Caught in a foamy swirl of branches and the carcass of a dead deer, he forced himself upward with a giant heaving thrust. His hand found a ledge to grip, a hunk of granite holding firm against the flood. He crawled, scraping against rock, arching his body onto the boulder where he clung, gasping for air.

Just ahead, he spotted Beaver twisted around the jutting branches of a pine tree. Out of breath, his heart racing, he tried to run toward him, but his leg gave way. Dragging and cursing his bad leg, he realized that Beaver wasn't holding on. His battered body was impaled on the broken branches. A rattlesnake was wrapped around Beaver's shoulder and neck.

He slid back into the rushing water, propelling him toward Beaver. Snake eyes fixed upon him. When the terrified snake struck, Tracker felt the impact. Fangs embedded. Deep. Lower abdomen. He grabbed the snake behind the head and flung it to the shore. In a flash of lightning he saw the snake's head, mouth wide open.

He slowly lifted Beaver's torso, and pulling with all his strength, managed to get the lifeless body to high ground. Blood flowed from deep gashes in Beaver's face, his eyes frozen wide open.

As Tracker gently lowered the body to the ground and stood back, he was immediately seized by a volley of pain in his own leg. And his abdomen. He grabbed his gut. Felt the watch, partially open. Dented. Still working. Lodged at the hinge of the watch, a fang.

His eyes dilated. No puncture wound in his skin. No blood. The watch...

Minutes passed before he was able to lift and carry Beaver up river to the camp.

Kate was the first to see him struggling and ran to him through the rain. She placed her fingers on Beaver's neck, feeling for a carotid pulse. Nothing.

10

"Mr. T, my family is on the other side. On the Ruidoso River. I've got to get to Clara," said J.C. He wasn't pleading, he was on the edge of panic. "The worst is over, I think. I can see some of the swing bridge is out, but if I can make it over, I can get help."

"Go," said Tracker.

"Take us, J.C.," said Kate.

"Please," added Izzie.

Tracker closed his eyes, said again, "Go."

Hands shaking, teeth chattering, Tracker tried to light the lantern, but dropped the match, which rolled between the planks and disappeared. He was sopping wet. On the porch in front of his headquarters, he paced, right hand in his pocket. It was broken, bones broken in several fingers. Nails blackened, one nail ripped out. Blood oozed through the wet handkerchief Kate had tightly wrapped in place. His boots were gone, shirt and vest in tatters. One sock. It wouldn't be light for hours. He had to get his bearings, size up the situation.

Then he remembered Beaver had been on the roof earlier in the day. He found the ladder by the back door, threw it against the wall, cursing his hand, ducking pieces of adobe plaster dislodged from above.

Using the strength of his upper body and one arm, he clawed his way on to the roof, stumbled over a roll of tar paper, fell to his knees. There was a gash high on his cheekbone. He didn't notice, concentrating on the state of the POW camp in the repeated millisecond lightning flashes.

He pulled himself to the parapet wall. He could barely hear a vehicle grinding toward him. A jeep, windshield down, was approaching the prison gates. The outline of a border patrolman, rifle pointed straight ahead, was silhouetted on the hood. In the beam of the headlights, he could see four handcuffed POWs marching in front of the vehicle.

He gave a two-fingered whistle. P I Maxwell, looked up, called out, "Sir, we caught all of them. Just outside Coalora, mile and a half west of Capitán."

"Must've been heading for the coal train."

"My guess, too, sir. My horse tracks like a dog. First thing I found were wrappers—the ones the German government sent them—Vitamin C wrappers. Fifteen minutes later I had them. Pretty stupid."

"Do I know any of them?"

"One, Müeller, the cook."

"Put all of them in solitary. Now!"

"For how long, sir?"

He arched his back in an attempt to ease the spasm in his leg. He needed aspirin. "I have no idea."

The cells were built before his arrival. A recently incarcerated hard-core Nazi had attacked one of the Columbus crew, nearly killing the sailor. The holding cells were situated dead center in the camp. Thick wooden timbers caulked with concrete chink formed the walls of each windowless five-by-five-foot cell. A small gap in the corrugated tin roof allowed a bare minimum of ventilation. A quart of water doled out once a day; a chamber pot three times a day. Conditions verging on inhumane.

He didn't remember crawling down the ladder. Hands shaking, he managed to get a lantern lit. He was filthy, hurt bad. He leaned over the basin, splashed frigid water on his face. Ugly bruise above his eye. Besides his broken hand, both arms were scraped raw. His rib cage was a mass of bruises and ached like the dickens. Even breathing hurt.

He gingerly pulled on a fresh shirt. His uniforms hung in the closet. Beaver must have moved his clothes to the new quarters before the storm. The poor man. This building was the last thing on earth that Beaver built.

No one at headquarters. The radio was dead. He slumped wearily in his desk chair, mind blank, eyes fixed on the steno pad. Shoved it in the desk drawer. He looked out into the mist. Fog hung over the camp. He lifted his left arm to the table top, cradled his head, passed out.

When he awakened, the ground fog was dissipating. Not direct light, but an ambient reflected light imbued everything. He lifted his head, wincing in pain. He was freezing. His hand shook as he lifted the receiver. Surprisingly, it still worked.

"Number please," said the operator.

"Sixty-five AJ."

"Marine Hospital."

"Kate..."

She recognized his voice. "We made it. J.C. was like a monkey, he made it over and got help. Planks were washed-out on the hospital side. He and a janitor managed to slide a ladder over the gap. We were on hands and knees. The chains held." She paused. "Are you okay? You looked so..."

Silence from Tracker. He heard the worry in her voice. Finally he said, "I feel like I'm coming out of a coma. Not sure what's real. Like I'm testing myself. Like a cautious cat. I'm not sure I slept. Maybe some. I am so damned tired, Kate."

Her voice was so soft, he could barely hear her. The tone, more than the words, flooded him with calm. Like his world was entering subsistence. Very gradually, Kate was willing his pain, mental and physical, to leave his body. He closed his eyes. He told her his men had carried Beaver's lifeless body to the barn. Maxwell had padded a quiet corner with fresh hay. Laid out a border patrol blanket. Together they carefully placed Beaver on the soft wool. Tracker had closed Beaver's eyes, crossed his arms over his chest, folding one dark hand over the other.

The sound of boots hitting the wood floor by the entrance startled Tracker. He straightened up, steadied his grip on the receiver. "Kate, J.C. just came in, hold for a second." When he came back on he told Kate that J.C. said that Clara and the baby were okay. They had moved to higher ground. "He says the water is down. I'm going to bring Beaver over myself." Click.

J.C. had already gathered Beaver's belongings. Extra uniform. Boots. Medal of Honor. A silver watch and seventy-five cents.

Tracker touched the medal. "This belonged to his father. He served in the 57th U.S. Colored Infantry," said Tracker. "We'll bury it with him. Help me move him."

"Want a pack horse?" J. C. asked.

"No. Current might be too strong. Lay him across my pommel and I'll ride piggyback. You ride ahead. Maxwell can take the rear."

Beaver's body safely transported to the morgue, Tracker sent the men back to the camp. Tracker rounded the hospital building, taking the steps one-by-one, limping down the hall, spotting Kate just as she sat down at her desk. She was still in the clothes from the night before. Makeup gone. Hair frizzled in curls. Fatigue obvious in her pale face.

She greeted him with a mug of hot tea and two aspirin. Her hands were unsteady. "By the looks of you, you need more than that crutch."

"I sure do." Unshaven, beat-up and bloody, no wonder she could read his mind. He settled stiffly into the armed wood chair next to her desk and stretched out his bad leg.

"I'm right here, Tracker, talk to me. And, I'm not going to leave."

A vein stood out on the left side of his temple. He pulled out a handkerchief and blew his nose. "That was tough. Poor Beaver. Drew a bad card in the deck. Makes me sick."

"Had you known him long? I could tell you really liked him."

"Not long, but somehow intense. Something palpable. I can't explain it. There's been so much going on since I arrived, and that man treated me like he cared."

"What would you expect?"

"Certainly not like that. Remember, this is a military job. No room to be much more than obedient." Tracker sipped the tea. He noticed his fingernails were dirty. Kate noticed it, too. "I have lost a man. I have lost a prisoner. I may lose my job over this."

"No! No self-doubt! Don't second guess yourself or anyone else."

"I'm an investigator, not a baby sitter. I grew up with no bathroom at home. Everyone was the same. Thirty-five dollars a week during the Depression, and damn glad to have it. Flying shows are on their way out. Last year was one of the worst years on record. For me and our country."

"Ever the skeptic, Tracker. Listen, one thing that is going to save you is your imagination."

He grunted, set down the mug of tea. "More like preservation."

"You're here to see Dr. Stillington, not me, or in addition to me?"

Tracker cocked his head as if not understanding. "Uh, no. Well, yes." He remained motionless in the chair for what seemed an awfully long minute. Distracted. Confused. Was it a concussion or was it her?

Kate shuffled a stack of charts, stacked them neatly. "Is there something else I can help you with?"

"I'll wait for the doctor," he said, wincing as he shifted.

"Is it your leg, is that why you're here? Let me see your hand."

"I got pretty bunged up last night—I hurt everywhere. I was hoping Dr. Stillington..."

"Might I take a look?" She checked her watch. "The roads are impassable. Arroyos had to run. With the bridge out, he'd have to drive all the way to Hondo and come from the east to get here. Would you trust me to take a look?"

He shook his head. Unconvincingly.

"I *am* a licensed nurse. I cover for the doctor when he's out." She

paused, a calculated pause, then said, "Look, this hospital is full of men."
He still didn't respond. Kate laughed, a big, open laugh. "I think our senior
patrolman is shy! Come on, let's get you in an exam room."

Tracker found himself leaning against the exam table. Kate lifted an
eyebrow. Obviously she was enjoying this. She had him by the balls and he
couldn't think of a way out. But did he really want to?

"I can't do much for your leg if I can't see it, Tracker. Drop your trousers." She turned her back, adding, "Besides, I've already seen everything
you have to offer."

Tracker had his hand on his belt buckle but stopped. Damn! She was
the one on that horse up above the cemetery. She had watched as he peed
circles in the dirt.

The muddy Levis came to rest in a tangled pile on his old work boots.
His hands were sweating and he hated that. His government-issue drab
green boxer shorts seemed very, very transparent. He didn't dare look at
the source of his real pain: his shriveled, still-healing limb.

Her pronouncement was distinctly clear. "*That* needs to be exercised."
"What?"

"You need PT—physical therapy. Don't look so shocked. You need to
build up those muscles in that leg, some sort of ankle weights, deep-knee-
bends. A steady regimen of pain killers wouldn't hurt, either. Never let the
pain get ahead of you. You tough guys always overdo things." She laughed.

"This is *not* funny."

"Lay down, let me flex it. Your leg, silly boy. Let me massage that
muscle. You need stimulation. Get that blood flowing. Trust me, I have
great hands."

•••

To her surprise Tracker had submitted to her demands. That was
quite something. While massaging and flexing his leg, she noted that even
with all the current atrophy, his muscles were still strong.

11

Paul led his exhausted paint horse into the barn. With all the humidity, the scent of fresh bales of hay competed with the smells seeping from the stalls. The air was hazy, soft, gray tonalities, like a platinum print.

For no reason at all, Paul remembered his mother, a Mescalero, bathed in such a monochrome light. He was a half-breed. It never bothered him, or her. She had told him that anyone treating him with condescension was ignorant. A petite woman, especially for an Apache, she was never angry with him. She had no temper. Instead, she would act disappointed. It always worked.

His mother, Sisika, or Little Bird, was a wise woman. She told him to make his time here on earth peaceful. She said her marriage ceremony was sacred. Peaceful. Everyone was there. A beautiful day. She loved it. A silver print of them reflected that love. Respect.

He released the cinch, reached for the horn and cantle and lifted his saddle. Swung it onto a rack in the tack room. Hung the bridle above it. Filled a halter bag with oats, gently lifted it over the horse's ears. Opened a stall door, patted the horse's rump, clicked to her, and the tired paint walked inside.

The shadowed figure of Grafton appeared in the haze. He looked bad, an unhealthy pallor. He leaned against a rugged support beam, and said, "Paul, I'm sorry to send you back out. But, my Jesus, that storm was so bad. Get a fresh mount and ride the whole damn flood plain." Paul had worked side-by-side with the other cowboys all night and half the morning, rescuing sheep and cattle. "I know you're bone-tired, but I don't trust anyone else."

∎∎∎

As the temperature rose, there was a pervasive smell of rot. Green slime already beginning to grow. Turning in the saddle to look back at the mountain, Tracker could see the peak was still shrouded. He edged the Appaloosa into a trot, passing a unit of prisoners pulling the remains of the bridge from the muddy water.

J. C. waved at him, his other hand on the rifle braced against his saddle horn.

"Poor Beaver. What a terrible way to die," said Tracker, pulling up beside him.

J. C. made the sign of the cross above his chest. *Vaya con Díos, mi amigo.* He couldn't look at Tracker. "What about burial?"

"Guess we better check with headquarters."

"Mr. T, he didn't have any family."

"Thought he did."

"Beaver had a habit of talking in the present. He told me—over a beer at the WPS in Ruidoso—that he lost his father in the First World War."

"I knew that."

"His mother died years ago, a heart attack."

"Was he married?" asked Tracker.

"Married to his job."

"He was a fantastic cook. A fine man. We'll do him right, have the service on the hill."

"How's your hand?" asked J.C.

"Hurts like hell, but what part of me doesn't? More important, how are Clara and the little one?"

"A neighbor got them out of any danger, took them up to their cabin. Big damage higher up in the canyon. Huge boulders, trees ripped out. Wiped out all the bridges in the village, swept through that plain by the racetrack. Our old cabin stood up pretty well. Tin roof. But the road is washed out. Only way in is by horseback or foot."

"Any deaths?"

"I heard a man was killed at Cedar Creek. His delivery truck stalled out in a low spot, water swept him away. He drowned. I'm afraid some of those farms along the Hondo might have seen flooding."

"The men got the perimeters secured mighty quick. Good job, them working all night in the dark. Give'em my compliments."

"Will do, Mr. T."

A truck arrived with a load of beams and lumber. POWs immediately began unloading, taking orders from one of their own.

"Pretty fast delivery," said Tracker.

"Got them from the Mescaleros. Place called Blazer's Mill on the rez. That German with the rip saw is the ship's engineer."

"I'm heading downstream. Check things out. If you need me, fire a round." With a cluck to his horse, he followed the alluvial plain, an undulating swirl of reddish-ochre mud that extended past the riverbank. He spotted the cow he had seen the night before; the carcass trapped in a tangle of uprooted piñons. The Appaloosa's hooves sucked, slipped in the sediment. Sinking in the mud up to its shanks.

Back at the bridge, he whistled at J. C., calling, "Tell Maxwell to take over. Let's get back to the camp."

An hour later, J.C. poked his head into the office. "Mr. T, I just checked on the autopsy of Beaver. The doctor's finished. Said he needed the space. Wants to know if he can call the mortician in Carrizozo."

"Yes. He needs the space?"

"A patient died, TB."

"Anything about the autopsy—I'm sure Beaver had severe internal injuries, right?"

"His neck was broken, pelvis, too. Two snakebites. Neck and face."

"Christ," said Tracker. "You got any whiskey around here?"

"Tequila."

"That'll do."

J.C. poured two shot glasses. Raised his glass in unison with Tracker. "To Beaver, *un hermano valiente.* Brave brother, there's no prejudice in Heaven."

There were bluish bags under Tracker's eyes. Skin the color of dirty dishrags. "I've been thinking. I grew up like most kids. Curious. Read a lot. Made A's and got beat up."

"You were smart," said J. C.

"No. Wise. At least for a teenage boy. I saw greed and avarice. Bigotry. I could read what kind of asshole would stand in front of poor people— black, brown, white—and look down on them. One guy in particular in Colorado," mused Tracker. "'Work'em was one of his favorite phrases. As if the term 'them' was part of the machine that made money. If the cog slipped, slowed things down, that cog was thrown away." Tracker shook his head, clearing his mind.

"J. C., I've been a cog in many a wheel."

A silence settled between them. J.C. poured them another shot. Tracker swallowed, cleared his throat. "Get on the radio. Tell them I'll have a full report soon, but right now I need to know if there's a certain protocol for Beaver's funeral. I want it done properly. Polish every boot, every saddle, breast collar. Dress uniforms. Full honors."

"Right, Mr. T."

When J.C. returned, Tracker was thinking out loud. "There has to be evidence in the camp. Spattered blood. A scuffle. Some place recently cleaned up. This was a fight to the death. Schmidt didn't just lie down and wait for his assailant to mutilate him."

J. C. and four other border patrolmen had done an extensive search on Saturday, finishing before the storm began. "I left the guard duties to the local-hires, used our own men for the search."

"And?"

"Nothing. Nothing at all, Mr. T."

"And now the flood has washed away anything you might have missed. Keep close tabs on the captain. And Müeller. That cook had access to a weapon that could puncture. He also knew Schmidt before they were shipmates. And he ran when he had the chance."

●●●

Chin resting on her hands, Kate wondered how Izzie had managed to stay on duty all night. Izzie didn't like to talk about herself much. But that afternoon they had spent at a bar in Ruidoso had been most revealing. They had gone to the Win-Place-Show Bar, right in mid-town. It was pre-racing season for the amateur track. The village was filling up with quarter horse owners. An influx of older summer people. No young men. All able bodies were in both theaters of a world at war.

Thinking about that afternoon, Kate remembered how Izzie had just opened up, like taking a lid off a Mason jar. There's a 'pop' as the pressure shield gives way. Izzie's story poured forth. An intelligent student, she had been chosen for a DAR scholarship in nursing. A Caring Ministries Nursing Scholarship. Her first bus ride was all the way to Philadelphia. She felt guilty. Her father had died in a head-on collision on the reservation. Her mother was devastated, but there was a younger brother who would take care of her and their sheep. Izzie wrote letters to their Mennonite priest who, in turn, would read them to Mrs. Jahata. The priest didn't tell Izzie that her brother, as a conscientious objector, (Hopis are People of Peace) had been imprisoned in Arizona. Sentenced to hard labor.

But her story wasn't finished. The Jahatas had more to endure.

Izzie told Kate about a stupid, inane Federal law call the Hopi Livestock Reduction Plan. The Feds decided the Hopi lands were overgrazed. Their insane solution: the Bureau of Indian Affairs slaughtered one half of every herd. Ordered by the director himself. A senseless waste.

Kate had asked about grounds for imprisoning the brother. Izzie told her the Hopis were caught, trapped by a bizarre entanglement of law versus religion. The tribe had been granted US citizenship in 1924, thereby making them subject to taxes, and the draft.

Izzie's mother died of complications from diabetes.

A small dust devil stirred up the dirt outside the bar. Kate remembered it because Izzie had lifted her head to look at it. Her profile filled with strength, backlit from the sunlit street. Kate would never forget the slow pace of Izzie's next words. She said that her brother had been released as a humanitarian gesture.

He had walked from Phoenix to Hotevilla-Bacavi, then to the family home near Oraibi. Two-hundred-and-fifty miles. On foot. The sheep were either dead or dying. He went on a binge, drinking until he blacked out. He was run over by a truck on Arizona State Route 264 in the night. The driver never knew it.

Izzie had graduated from the Pennsylvania Hospital in Philadelphia in January, 1941, and joined the Army Nurse Corps. Fort Stanton Marine Hospital was her first posting.

...

Kate had spent hours helping the ambulatory patients in the tents on the hill above the hospital. Piling sandbags, shoveling mud, delivering dry clothes, blankets, hot food, meds. Pneumonia was always around the corner. The men had weathered the storm; two half-wall tents had suffered flood damage. They weren't as lucky at the hospital. A patient had died in the night, a young sailor from Michigan. Everyone was jumpy, especially Anderson, day three after the pneumothorax.

Kate waved to the janitor mopping up water in Ward 1. "Bill, God bless you. The ladder saved us. And you and J.C. got the generator running. You're our hero."

"Anytime, Miss Kate. It was really the border patrolman that got it running. Knows his way around engines, that's for sure."

She crossed the hall to Anderson's bed. "How're you feeling today? You're handling the breathing better, I can tell." She pulled a chair alongside the bed. If possible, he appeared more pale than ever. "Like all the sailors here, I bet you've got quite a story."

"Want to hear it?" he asked, taking shallow, labored breaths.

Kate prodded him with a tilt of her head. "I'm all ears, and besides, it gives me a chance to get off my feet."

"I'm from a family of mariners. Dad and my granddad both, too. Worked the Great Lakes." He hesitated, closed his eyes. In a voice barely audible, he told her he saw merchant ships carrying oil get hit. He said the whole load goes at once. Two-thousand-feet-high. Fire cloud. Lights the sky for miles. Nothing's left. When it burns off. He gasped for air.

Kate placed a finger to her lips. "No more talking."

Anderson shook his hand. "I want to tell you."

With reticence, she leaned forward. His speech came in spurts, spaced between minutes of compensating rapid-breathing. He told her he didn't hear the torpedo hit his Liberty ship. Knocked off his feet. A wall of flame. Cargo. Tanks. Ambulances. Troop carriers. Spilled like marbles. A gaping hole. Portside. All sucked down. Like a giant whirlpool.

Men were flung from the listing deck. He managed to dive into the burning water. Immediately forced downward. Downward current. He kicked hard, spun in the water, looked back. The Liberty ship was vertical. Then a thunder-like crack. The ship broke in two.

Eight minutes. She fell keel-first beneath the waves.

The back of his shirt was on fire. He had kicked like a wild man. Three men survived. Two hours in the icy water. Rescued by a Royal Navy warship. Had his ship taken the usual North Sea route, they would have frozen to death.

A German plane had been sighted. No escort. American convoys were sitting ducks. No guns. Telephone poles painted grey. Looked like cannons. Three million tons of shipping. Lost. A sense of fatigue hung heavily over both. His story was like so many. She heard grisly descriptions. Limbs lost. Eyes blinded. Lives changed forever. In two years at the mariner hospital, she had witnessed twenty-five deaths. Number twenty-six would be no easier.

●●●

When the ship's bell rang, Tracker looked at his pocket watch; it was twelve noon. An unfamiliar patrolman was at the stove. He wasn't hungry and he wasn't ready to meet the new cook. He left.

12

A tired, sweaty group of German prisoners on foot were being escorted back into the prison compound. As the huge, cyclone wire-topped gates swung back, Tracker recognized the ship's engineer. J.C. followed the POW's on horseback. When he saw his boss, he hopped down, tied his horse to the hitching rail beside the Appaloosa.

"Lunch, Mr. T ?"

"Not hungry." He popped two aspirin in his mouth.

"Got burritos in my saddle bag."

"That's different. I always can eat one of Clara's. You know, I've been wondering what the flood did to that swimming pool. Let's ride up there and take a look from the fence line."

Tracker pulled himself up in the saddle with his left hand. Winced, signaled something to Maxwell, headed west, then turned south, climbing as they rode. "Tell me what you know about the pool."

"It was Daehne's idea. Olympic size. State of the art engineering," said J.C. He had learned about the project from his predecessor. He told me the Germans knew what they were doing. They had a team of technicians that took care of the pool on their ship. Knew all about filtration, chlorination, heating unit, even underwater lighting.

The Germans weren't considered prisoners at the time, merely wartime detainees. That was 1940. They dug and dug, built wooden frames, poured concrete batch by batch. It was fed by spring water, and put through a purifying system. They knew to use chlorine to oxidize the bacteria and algae, kept watch on the pH. J.C. had heard there was only one small problem the first summer. Copper in the water. The techs used an algaecide. All of the blond guys' hair turned green.

Tracker laughed. "What did they do?"

"Vinegar."

Tracker stopped abruptly. "Here's a good spot. Time for burritos."

"Yes, sir."

They dismounted next to the spring that fed the now-brown pool below. The horses took a long drink, began grazing. Tracker propped himself against a huge granite boulder, cool to the touch. Took the burrito offered to him. "First moment of peace and quiet in the last 24 hours."

"Ain't that the truth."

"Best burrito I've ever eaten, J.C."

"My mother taught Clara how to fix frijoles. There's a trick—don't let them burst. Keep the liquid clear. Salt pork. Takes three-plus hours. I grew up in a little tiny town outside of Las Cruces, place called Tortugas. Spanish for "turtle." Maybe that's why I'm so slow."

"Slow? That you are not."

"We had this baseball team. My mom made frijoles and enchiladas for the whole team. Everyone came after the game. Had a ball."

"You any good?"

"Sliding bases."

"Stealing bases."

J.C. chuckled. "Yeah. You know that Mexico owned all of this." J.C. gestured expansively. "My ancestors. Their land was taken, stolen by banks, lawyers. Ever heard of the Treaty of Guadalupe Hidalgo?"

"Heard, but don't know any details," said Tracker.

"Well, they taught us all about it where I lived, so close to the Rio Grande. It was the peace treaty signed in 1848, ended the Mexican-American War. It added 525,000 square miles to United States Territory. All or most of what is now Arizona, New Mexico, California, Colorado, Nevada. And don't forget, Utah and Wyoming."

"My Lord. Really?"

"Yup. The treaty recognized the once mighty Rio Grande as the southern border of the United States."

"Always knew you were pretty sharp. Let's give it up and get back to work," Tracker said, straightening the flat brim of his hat.

■■■

"What's playing tonight?" asked J. C.

"Ah, *The Mummy*," answered Maxwell, unpacking the reel.

"Saw that over in Roswell about ten years ago when it came out. You're on the main gate tonight, right?"

"Yep, just my luck. Hey, this thing's got Boris Karloff in it," said Maxwell.

"That'll spook'em. Stop them griping about Müeller in solitary. Those Krauts live to eat. Hope Mr. T knows what he's doing."

"Spoiled bunch of bastards, if you ask me," Maxwell muttered.

"How would you know? Everything you cook tastes like licking a salt block."

Maxwell took a rifle out of the gun case. "True, but you swallow those *jalapeños* like they were green beans. Going to burn up your insides."

"*Muy macho.* Makes hair grow on your chest. I'm going home for dinner, and be back later. I'll bring you an *empanada.* Finish the paperwork on the breakout, then radio headquarters."

∎∎∎

Standing in the kitchen, deep in conversation with Izzie, subjects abstract, intermixed, comfortable, Kate wondered aloud, "Do you know much about J.C.?"

"Not much, bits and pieces. It's obvious that Tracker has known him for a long time. He's the godfather to J.C.'s daughter, Linda. And, he was part of J.C. and Clara's wedding. Best man."

"When did you hear that?"

"You heard it, too. Remember when J.C. told us he would be bringing his old patrolman buddy up from El Paso to take over. Agent Dodds was his best man."

"Must have been busy."

"Kate, you've been too busy playing around with Mr. T to really listen."

"Playing around?"

"Cigarette breaks together. Horseback riding. You don't think I don't notice."

The small kitchen seemed even smaller to Kate. Izzie asked her for the bag of blue cornmeal. "I thought you had it. Want another beer, Izzie?"

∎∎∎

Tracker parked the mud-spattered jeep at the southeast corner of the fort. The hospital, centered on the north side of the parade field, was already lit up. The nurses' quarters on the southeast corner as well. The two-story ivy-covered stone headquarters building sat imposing but silent on the east side. He crossed the quadrangle to Stillington's quarters opposite the headquarters. Drapes drawn. A sliver of light. Seven o'clock on a Sunday night. He knocked on the door, the light of the screened-in porch clicked on. Stillington appeared, his shirtsleeves rolled up, flowery tie loosened.

"Believe you lent it to the girls last night," Tracker said, handing him the broken red-and-white striped umbrella. "Wind got it, I'm afraid."

"I had forgotten about it," Stillington said absently.

Over the doctor's shoulder to the right of the reception hall, Tracker could see a glass-fronted cabinet lined with liquor bottles. A silver martini shaker sat on a tray, frosted with moisture. An oriental carpet on the wood floor. Classical music playing somewhere in the background.

"Nice place, Doctor."

"Um. Yes. Built in eighteen seventy-seven. In the military years, this was the Commanding Officer's quarters. The architect for the fort must have come from the east coast."

Tracker looked closer for the first time. Each building had thick whitewashed rock walls, spick-and-span, military-style. Second-story dormers. Palladian windows here and there. Arched walkways covered with ivy and Virginia creeper.

"Something you would see on the coast of Maine. Certainly not the usual adobe that's so prevalent here. It's way too large for me. There's a huge kitchen, formal dining room. Another dining room for the staff. I would guess the wife was glad to have these rock walls and officer's quarters on both sides while her husband was out fighting Apaches."

Tracker leaned on the door frame. Stillington stepped back. "Looks like I caught you working. Hope it's the report on Schmidt."

"No, I'm still waiting on Santa Fe. I expect something tomorrow or Tuesday."

"I'll be in your office first thing. I suggest you get on the horn and light a fire under those people up north. Have them wire the results. I need that report. Headquarters in El Paso is breathing down my neck."

Tracker stepped back, walked away into the darkness. It was a moonless night, though there was a glow emanating from the prison lights across the river. As he cut diagonally across the parade field, visions of uniformed cavalry marching in unison filled his mind. Nearly ninety years of military history in this place, now Tracker Dodds was the one in uniform. Not after Apaches, but after a murderer.

He found himself in front of the nurses' quarters. Unlike the other buildings, it was pueblo style. A couple of knocks.

Kate appeared, beer in hand, silhouetted against the porch lights. Her hair was parted down the middle. She was barefooted. Wrapped in a short Chinese silk robe.

With just one look, Tracker knew she was drunk.

"Come in, stay for dinner," Kate said, "Izzie's cooking."

•••

Sunday, movie night. The prisoners milled about before they chose spots on the hill beyond the swimming pool. Mounted guards outside the fence watched. The German officers made no effort to control the men. Grumbling. Tightknit groups. An occasional loud voice. Almost as loud as the pigs squealing down by the feed silos. Across the way, steam emanated from the laundry. Warm spots of light appeared in the dormer windows above. Sunday evening.

The projector light focused on the makeshift screen. Flickering frames. Choppy voice cuts crackled. *The March of Time* newsreel began. A technician from the *Columbus* crew tightened the focus, adjusted the sound. Black and white images of rows of merchant ships. A destroyer left a wide wake of foaming water. Barrage balloons overhead, daring German aircraft. Their tethered steel cables were capable of slicing wings, shattering propellers.

The voice-over announced: "Another convoy reaches our British allies. Soon there will be an unbeatable assemblage of men and equipment to attack and sustain a front, driving the Hun back to their caves." The dialogue was drowned out by angry booing and catcalls. The image of the most protected of all merchant ships, an American tanker, appeared, then suddenly erupted in a glowing inferno of fuel oil. The U-boat's torpedo had struck midship. The voice-over echoed across the meadow: "Shipping losses immediately off our own coasts are mounting. Nearly one-hundred-and-twenty allied ships were lost in May, thousands of lives lost to the deep." Some of the audience roared with approval, clapping in unison over their heads.

Captain Daehne, as well as his officers, sat stiffly in their chairs, looking straight ahead.

***

Tracker stepped inside the small shared apartment. A fan turned slowly.

"Wanna beer?" Kate asked, turning down the radio. "The guys from the *Columbus* band—they can play this stuff, you know, like Count Basie, Artie Shaw. We should get them to play for our patients." She moved a stack of *Collier's* and old *Post* magazines, clearing a place for him on the couch.

Tracker sat down, picked up a stack of photos laying next to a lamp with a fringed shade. Pluck settled at his feet.

"That's me, my high school class photo, Wyoming-style," Kate said, pointing to a skinny girl sitting on the ground in the front row, legs crossed. "We were trading memories," she added, shuffling through the black and white photos. "Look at Iz back on the rez. Isn't she a beauty."

Izzie turned away from the stove to smile briefly at them. "I was sixteen. Maiden ritual."

"Amazing," said Tracker, looking at the statuesque young woman in full Hopi regalia. "You were—are—very lovely."

Izzie let his remark go, saying instead, "My *poovol piki* is my favorite. I make it just like my grandmother." She served Tracker first. "Blue corn. I grind it up, make dumplings. We call them 'blue marbles.' I added a little kick."

"I can take it—ten years living on the Border," said Tracker. He took a large spoonful.

"When meat is scarce, this stew is very satisfying." She emptied her bowl, licked it clean. A very sexy Indian, Tracker thought.

Kate looked at her watch. "Almost time, I'll turn it on." The crackling cleared as she adjusted the dial on the Victrola console.

"Good evening, America," said President Roosevelt. "It is nine-thirty PM eastern war time. My fellow countrymen, it is my sad duty to report..."

Kate snapped off the radio. "Headlines of doom. Bad news, good music, the story of forty-two. The world's gone crazy." She slid a record from the sheath, tossed the album cover to Tracker. The ten-inch wide shellac 78 RPM disk played for only four minutes a side, but what a ride. She drew on her cigarette. "Dorsey's good for the digestion."

"So is my tea," Izzie called from the kitchen.

Before he could ask, Kate said, "Izzie's special brew. For hard times she brings out her stash."

Izzie held up a bundle of sticks. "Hopi tea. Also called cota or green-thread. Grows back home all over the Four Corners region for a very short time during the monsoon season. You can re-use the boiled herb. When we gather, it is important to say a prayer. Explain to the plant why it is being moved. If you don't, the balance..." Tracker picked up the chant-like rhythm of her voice. Izzie words went on, "And harmony of Mother Earth is broken. We take the herb from all four directions to keep the balance. Never take more than you can use. Leave some behind with a prayer of thanks. Mother Earth will continue to bear her fruits.

"Just as the bright yellow flower buds open, cut it three inches from the soil. Take a string—I use the string off a bag of Blue Bird Flour. Take two stalks. Fold about four inches from the root. Keep folding. Tie string around twice and knot like this one."

Izzie handed a cup to Tracker. "Takes away the pain. I know for certain." He took a sip. "Tea for you, Kate?"

"Not tonight, Iz." She poured a thimble of rum into a glass, and a splash in Tracker's tea. "Got this in Juárez. Bacardi. It is divine."

Several records had dropped from the stack by the time *All of Me* began to play. Kate's fingers toyed with the collar of her robe. She stood suddenly, then fell back on the couch. "Oops," she said, rising slowly, this time in a broad-legged stance. "Iz, wanna dance?"

"Yes," Izzie said, her face soft, malleable.

The sound of *Boogie Woogie Bugle Boy* sent the girls into a jitterbug, bumping the walls, almost falling over the table, catching each other. Pluck barked grumpily, and retreated to Kate's bedroom. They all burst out laughing.

The girls were a long way from a hospital, the war-torn patients. Tracker sipped his spiked tea. No pain in his leg. Or his hand. Or anywhere.

"Hey, big guy," laughed Kate, shuffling towards him. "Come on, dance with us. That pretty face, that strong body...I bet you're real good." As an afterthought, she added, "Remember: exercise."

Tracker reached for her hand and pulled her onto the overstuffed arm of the couch. "Sorry, pretty lady, yesterday did me in. Besides, I'd better get back to the camp."

"Not yet. We're dying to know what happened to your leg."

■■■

The images flickered. A large white caption superimposed over a sinking aircraft carrier read: JAPAN'S AKAGI NAGUMO'S FLAGSHIP, SUNK ALONG WITH HER SISTER, THE KAGA. In strident tones, the voice-over began, "Dive bombers from the Enterprise and Yorktown at the center of battle. June 4, 1942, the turning point of the war in the Pacific."

Close-ups of German soldiers dodging through ruins and billowing smoke, followed by the commentary, "Colonel-Generals von Kleis and Hoth continue their advance towards the Caucasus. General von Paulus continues undaunted toward Stalingrad."

No one seemed to notice the panzers burning in vaults of fiery death or foot soldiers crumpled in the snow. The devout Nazis in the camp were ready to fight about anything. A catcall from one of the *Columbus* crew was all it took. The code of discipline imposed by Captain Daehne disintegrated. Pushing. Shoving escalated into a fistfight.

Arms folded across his chest, Captain Daehne had his eyes on the mounted guards outside the fence.

The fistfights progressed into a vicious wrestling match. Men cheered, scattered, three men fell against the screen. The projector crashed down. The voice-over ground into the dirt with a whine.

13

"So, what happened to your leg?" Izzie asked, sitting down beside Tracker.

"I was on duty, out in the field in a jeep, when I first saw him."

He told them the low-flying Stinson L-5 almost clipped him. "This border patrol pilot was landing planes and getting airborne again in places no airplane belonged. Deserts. Ditch banks. Narrow canyons. Steep inclines. I knew I could do it. It's like barnstorming, but I would have a steady job."

"Get to the part about your leg, Tracker," said Kate impatiently.

"I got the job. My wings. I was flying patrol below El Paso near Zaragosa. Following the Rio Grande. Flying real low, parallel to a dirt road. Desolate. I saw a body underneath a bridge. Circled back. Landed on the levee. Ran down, found two men, both in bad shape, barely alive."

He had given them what water he had. Revived one of them enough to speak. In whispered Spanish, the man said three nights and days. No water. Temperature over one-hundred-degrees.

"I radioed for a jeep crew. Nearly dark. While the men were getting the poor guys on stretchers, I got back in my plane, but it wouldn't start. The battery was dead."

The ground patrol pulled the jeep alongside the Stinson. "I turned on the magnetos. We hooked up the jumper cables and I started manually pulling the propeller through. It started right up. The guys backed the jeep down from the levee real fast. I ran back to the jeep to return their cables. When I turned back to the plane, it had started rolling. It was going to take off. I knew right away the screw lock on the brake had vibrated loose. I jumped for the cockpit. My right leg got caught in front of the wheel. I went down. Underneath the plane."

"Oh, no," Kate said, suddenly more sober.

"I tried to stand up, get back in the cab, but I crumpled to the ground. The plane had broken my leg."

"What did you do?"

"I fainted."

•••

As Daehne expected, the guards were awaiting a signal. Their well-oiled rifles raised like long black daggers against the lingering light. The rifles seemed to float as each man took aim on the mob. Daehne didn't hear the curses flying among the men—he heard the sliding of bolt-actions chambering rounds. In precise, dogmatic German, he snapped to his aide, "Signal all crew to attention." The shrill sound of the boatswain's pipe pierced the air. Every single man saluted with *Sieg Heils*. All eyes turned toward Daehne, who pointed deliberately at the perimeter fence, the line of ready rifles.

Anger turned to unity. Hardcore Nazis and anti-Hitlerites became Germans. A terrifying rumbling. POWs surged in a convulsive wave. Faces contorted with hatred, they stormed the fence, screaming at the mounted guards. The sound became deafening. Horses reared back, eyes red-rimmed with panic.

Alarm blasts sounded throughout the valley. J. C. grabbed a canvas satchel full of canisters and face masks, jumped down the steps at head-quarters, hit the gravel in full sprint as the mob surged forward. "Where's Dodds!" he yelled to the gate guards.

"Gone, sir, the hospital," Maxwell yelled back.

"Shit! Give me your horse." Maxwell slid off just as J. C. wrapped the satchel over the saddle horn, swung into the saddle. "You," he yelled to the other mounted patrolman, "Go get Dodds. Tell him to get his ass back here."

■■■

Tracker fell silent, thinking back on the emergency hospitalization and surgery the next day. The bone surgeon had visited him shortly after returning to the ward from recovery. That had been one of the times he wished he hadn't recovered. The doctor's explanation of what he could expect during and after recovery had been devastating. The break wasn't that simple. Crush injuries exponentially complicated the damage. His leg would always be a source of trouble. He needed months of physical therapy. Intermittent, intense pain would dog him forever, whether overworking the leg or experiencing emotionally traumatic events. Tracker shook his head trying to clear his mind of the overwhelming despondence.

"That accident cost me my flying career in the Army. Worse, the two Mexicans died."

Through the screen door, they all heard the sound of alarm sirens screaming, reverberating, shrill as a blade cutting through granite. Tracker was out the door, saw the patrolman running across the parade ground toward him.

"Sir! Riot!"

●●●

J. C. quickly handed canisters to Maxwell. "Tear gas. Use it. You know the plan. Get your mask on. Get'em back from the fence." He urged his horse forward in an arc around the perimeter, tossing canisters, masks to each mounted patrolman. At his signal, the men vaulted the tear gas into the compound.

The mob surged toward the main gate, trying to escape the fumes. Charging inmates rammed the solitary cells. Clawing, kicking, battering the timbers. Müeller wedged his wiry torso through a gap in the wall, jerked his legs free. He ran for the gate, straight into Maxwell's volley.

Müeller was instantly blinded.

Captain Daehne was at his side immediately, trying to muffle the cook's screams. Müeller coughed, choked, threw up. Daehne tried to help him to his feet, but Müeller struck out, arms flailing. The captain went down, grinding his face in Müeller's vomit. Prisoners trampled past them, gagging, stumbling blindly. Tower guards fired shots in the air. Ominous cracking sounds. Daehne yelled to his crew to back down. In a more guttural tone, he ordered the Nazi POWs to stand at attention at arm's length.

A piercing whistle sounded. This time from J.C. His eyes on Daehne, he commanded the inmates to fall in at the sports field. He snapped at Maxwell, "Roll call—then lockdown."

The prisoners began to retreat in a semi-organized march. J. C. waited until they were all in formation, then dismounted. A voice came from behind him.

"I understand you asked for me," said Tracker.

14

J. C. and Maxwell dragged Müeller to the office. Tracker flushed his eyes repeatedly with sterile water. Wrapped heavy gauze over his eyes, around his head.

Müeller moaned, clenched fists at his side. "Blind...can't see. *Mein Gött in Himmel,* blind."

"Take off that filthy shirt, drop it on the floor." Tracker kneeled down to smell it. Besides the body odor, he could detect the faint odor of apple blossoms. "How old were those canisters, J. C.?"

"*Muy viejo,* Mr. T, very old."

Two nights before his section graduated from Camp Chigas, Tracker had seen for himself dangers of out-of-date chemical weaponry. During an undercover raid on a *colonia* in the upper valley of El Paso, a *coyote*—a smuggler—had thrown a gas canister directly into a border patrolman's face. Later, at the agent's bedside at Thomason Hospital, the physician explained that the broken-down active ingredient—crystalized chloroacetophenone—had caused severe iritus with temporary blindness. As a field surgeon in World War I, the doctor had seen many such incidents on the battlefields of France.

Tracker surprised himself for remembering the name of the chemical, but the event had been shocking. He would never forget the chemical smell clinging to his own uniform. He kicked the shirt toward Maxwell. "Throw this away, use a stick. Really wash your hands."

Drying his own hands at the sink, Tracker watched J. C. lead Müeller to a cot. The guy was a mess. Disoriented, blinded. Covered with vomit.

Tracker pulled a chair to the bed. The sound of the legs scraping the wooden floor in the near-barren room seemed unusually loud.

Müeller pushed himself against the headboard. "Who is it?"

Tracker sat in silence. Müeller kept turning his head, listening intently. Tracker didn't make a sound.

■■■

"Good morning, Maxwell. O—six-hundred," Tracker said. "Get going with muster and roll call. I'll write up the report for headquarters. Chief Vonshooven's going to chew my butt if I don't come up with some answers."

"Uh, sir. I have the chief on the phone right now," said Maxwell.

Tracker was on the phone immediately. "Agent Dodds, here, sir."

"You know I don't like excuses. This border patrol sector has been ordered to take care of the Fort Stanton POW camp by the Office of the Provost Marshall General. You're in charge of the first prisoner of war camp in this country. Don't embarrass the entire force. I'm giving you one week to solve the murder or I will replace you. Bury our man with full honors, and I don't want to hear any more problems." Click.

"A great start for Monday. He is really pissed-off. And he doesn't know about the riot yet. I'm heading for the showers."

"Hey, Mr. T, I'll do it," said J.C.

"The riot was my fault."

"No. It was coming. You know that." Tracker started to resist.

"Go take a shower," said J.C.

Bare-chested, his heavy beard as dark as his mood, he tossed a towel over his shoulder. Headed for the shower block. Feeling jumpy, nervous. The water pressure was okay but freezing cold. He liked it cold; maybe it would sharpen his senses.

He flexed the bad leg. Tried a deep knee bend. A little stronger. He was thin. Ribs showed. Hollow indentations in his pelvis. Gray hair on his chest. Muscles in his arms thicker than the bad leg. But his good leg was solid, like a tree. He chuckled. Yeah, solid like an ancient juniper tree. At least his sense of humor was coming back.

"Hey, Mr. T," J. C. called.

"Hey, yourself. Toss me that towel."

"Get any sleep?" Tracker asked, rubbing his hair with the towel. He pulled on his trousers and sat down on the bench beside J.C.

"Once I got that image of the gas hitting Müeller's face out of my mind."

"The bastard deserved it. His eyes will clear up."

"Want him back in solitary?"

"Not yet. I need a trouble-free day, haven't had one since I got here." He leaned his bare shoulders against the rough planks. His tanned face and hands were noticeably darker than his chest.

Maxwell exploded through the door. "Funeral guy's got Beaver's casket. Wants to have some help digging the grave up on Buffalo Ridge."

"Buffalo Ridge?" asked Tracker.

"It's a few miles from here. Beautiful spot," said J.C. "The Buffalo

Soldiers, the black troopers from the 9ᵗʰ Cavalry, were buried there."

Like a pressure cooker, Track asked with a rasp, "Not in the cemetery on the hill?"

"No."

Tracker growled. "The Jim Crow laws and lynching's in the South were the reasons I came out here. Sticks in my craw."

"My feelings, exactly," said Stillington from the doorway. "I petitioned to be-stationed here. I was raised by a Negro nanny. Quite well. I might add. However, my ex-wife was guilty of *de jure*, racial segregation. 'Separate but equal' actually meant African Americans were inferior."

"Beaver and the rest of us ate out of the same bean pot. I'm not giving some asshole undertaker the privilege to tell me where to bury him," snapped Tracker. "J.C., Maxwell, go down there, tell that bastard to put the casket in Doc's morgue and get his ass out of here. Okay with you, Doctor?"

"Of course. In my medical practice, the Negroes had their separate waiting room. I remember treating a New Orleans policeman after a riot in the Quarter. He was beat on pretty bad. I noticed blood on his truncheon. I asked him if there were any fatalities. You know what he said? 'Six dead, not counting Blacks and Mexicans.'" His shoulders dropped. "Beaver's mother was Catholic. I will call a priest that I know in Ruidoso. Tracker, I was looking for you because I may finally have something for you in my office."

"Let me get a clean shirt. I'll drive you back."

The jeep dropped down from the bridge in a muddy rut. Stillington motioned toward the elevator.

"No. I need the exercise," said Tracker, heading straight up the stairs.

Stillington's desk was strewn with medical journals. He handed an article from the *New England Journal of Medicine* to him.

Notes in the margin. *Not likely. All blood elements present. Possible to knock out just platelets?*

He turned to the title: *Genetic Blood Dyscrasias*. Stillington's next notation was difficult to read, but he thought a single capitalized word read: *ABERRATION???*

"I think I'm on the right track. Give me some more time," said Stillington.

●●●

Downstairs at the nurses' station, Tracker said, "Good morning, Miss MacAllan."

She looked up from the stack of charts with a startled look. "Sorry, I didn't see you come in. Is everything okay? The riot? You left so fast last night."

"Everything's settled down, but no thanks to me. Riot controlled. J. C. handled everything by the book."

"I'm curious. How long have you known Agent Chávez? You seem to trust him more than most people."

They had met in El Paso. Tracker had finished his junior year at Texas A & M, ran out of money. He heard the border patrol was interviewing. A patrol inspector made two-thousand dollars a year.

"After barnstorming for pennies at little county fairs, that was real money."

"Tell me more," said Kate.

•••

Tracker Dodds and Jimmy Chávez had both registered within minutes of each other at Hotel Vogel, 314 West Missouri Street in El Paso. $35 a month, room and board. The two of them joined the Border Patrol Cadet Corps the next morning. Three months before graduation, they were paired as a two-man team assigned to narcotics.

Tracker hesitated for a moment, trying to recall details, timing.

It was a hot summer night when they crossed the International Bridge into Juárez. Neon signs. *Cruz Blanca. Corona. Jose Cuervo. Bacardi.* Stooped Tarahumara Indians—all women—draped in *serapes*, faces hidden by flat-brimmed black hats. Barefoot. Begging. Curio stores, stalls selling gold and silver jewelry next to booths selling horse shit cigarettes. G. I.'s from Fort Bliss. Pretty much all about three things—drinking, drugs and prostitutes. Volstead Act be damned.

He remembered sitting in an upscale bar. They ordered tequila shooters. The waiter set them up with another round. J.C. had done the talking. Asked the waiter about a high-rolling poker game he had heard about. Tracker revealed a roll of bills inside his vest pocket. His buy-in. One-thousand dollars (courtesy of the border patrol).

A cigarette girl smelling of cheap perfume stopped by their table. Lucky Strikes, Camels. Pall Mall. The waiter backed away. Tracker headed for the men's room.

J.C. was waiting at the door. The waiter said the game was on. J.C. had provided Tracker's cover—he was an instructor pilot. He would be heading to the draft any day. The poker game was in a small back room. Green felt table, one overhead light. One outside exit.

Two bankers. A hotel manager. One woman. *Señora Barragán* had glossy black hair, ruby lips matching the color of her tight suit. Shoulder pads, definitely Mexican aristocracy. Probably in her fifties—reading glasses. Her dog rested his head on his front legs, eyes closed, beneath her chair.

The same waiter appeared. The *rico* from El Paso ordered a *ron Castillo con soda*. *Señora Barragán* the same. Nothing for the bankers. The tall banker from Torreon hummed when his hand was good. The short Jewish banker was sweaty.

At the break, the hotelier told Tracker that once the international trolleys extended to the Cassidy Gate at Fort Bliss, soldiers had flooded downtown El Paso and Juárez. Only six cents to ride anywhere.

The man allowed that Tracker was good at poker. Tracker's reply was the truth. He had been through the Depression and the Dust Bowl. Without a cent and no job in sight, he had to drop out of Texas A & M. He gambled to eat.

When the man asked if he had trained to fly at A & M, again Tracker answered with the truth. Army ROTC, Warrior Training Battalion, Corps of Cadets.

Back to poker. It was time for Tracker to attack.

The hotelier rubbed the back of his neck. He had the cards.

Señora Barragán folded. The bankers folded one after another.

Tracker was all in.

The hotelier tossed a gold pocket watch in to sweeten the pot. Raised, called. Full House.

Tracker lifted his eyebrows and exhaled. Spread his hand. Then he raised his hand like a butcher slamming a cleaver into a hunk of beef, signaling J.C. to lunge forward.

J.C. had his shirt partially unbuttoned. Swept the booty into his shirt. Pivoted. Ran. Head down.

The German Shepherd sprung. Across the table. Snagging Tracker's sleeve, drawing blood. The thrust of the dog's rear legs caused the table to smash backwards, knocking chairs to the floor.

Both zigzagged through the bar. Knocking over chairs, customers. Women screamed. Someone tripped J.C., but he didn't go down. A shot rang out, a barrage of bullets screamed wall-to-wall. Tracker ducked. Right. Left. Right. Jumped on a table, tucked into a tight ball, head down. Rolled explosively through the front window. Glass shards everywhere. Blood. Chaos. Horns blowing. Whistles. Clogged street. J.C. running, propelling a bloodied Tracker ahead of him. Trolley #54, destined for the Cassidy Gate, clanged, approaching as if in slow motion.

The trolley car was jammed with soldiers from Fort Bliss. Tracker dove for the double doors. J. C. milliseconds behind him. GIs dragged them on. Someone threw pennies into the open window of the tollbooth on the American side on Santa Fe Street. Rails sparked. Bells tinkled. #54 crossed into the United States.

Tracker remembered the chief at Camp Chigas had called their night of drinking and gambling in Juárez a 'boondoggle' in private, but their report had led to an investigation with cooperation from the FBI. And a commendation ribbon at commencement.

"Surprised?" asked Tracker, returning to the present. Kate nodded. "Yeah, surprised me, too."

15

"Do you happen to have a medical dictionary?" Tracker asked.

Kate replaced the cap on her fountain pen with a sharp click. Spun around in her secretarial chair. Handed him a heavy volume.

"I'll bring it back real quick."

Kate found herself staring at the door long after Tracker left. She felt somehow empty, or was it lonely? Was it the isolation of Fort Stanton, or the fact that most of the patients around her were debilitated, helpless. Far, far away from their loved ones. She had tried the love thing before. Twice. A brief marriage to a medical student when at nursing school. They shared a love for all things outdoors. His family owned a summer cabin in Creede, Colorado. The couple spent a blissful honeymoon there, not venturing out except for a night at the summer stock theater. Then it was back to work. Long hours and too many demands on each other's time eventually dampened the spark. The marriage fizzled.

Husband number two, a commanding trial-lawyer-turned-politician who gave his soul to the highest bidder. She couldn't take his false life. She left him and retreated into the U.S. Public Health Service, asking for a remote posting. The high altitude, the mountain climate, the clean air reminded her of Wyoming. At forty-six, she was her own woman, full of empathy for her patients, but wary of another attachment.

And as for Tracker Dodds? Chemistry—she didn't believe in it. Then why was she so taken by the tall, grey-haired guy? She began to wonder if she had gone overboard the night before. Why was he standing in the dark in front of her apartment by himself? He certainly didn't turn down her invitation to stay.

She picked up a pack of cigarettes, thought better of it, and walked out the front door of the hospital. The smell of fresh-mown grass filled the quadrangle; it was a great day for a picnic, or flying, for nearly anything. Why did she feel so restless? She recalled her father telling her to close her eyes and face the sun, tilted face up to absorb the full power of the light. It was the mantra she preached to each of her tuberculosis patients: the cleansing, rejuvenating power of the sun. Her face lifted, she felt the warmth soothe the tight muscles in her neck. She let her chin fall to her chest, slowly opened her eyes, blinking in the bright light. Bringing her vision into focus, she looked across the parade grounds and saw Tracker following Izzie inside the apartment.

∎∎∎

Tracker paced the floor of the small living room. "Do you know anything about scalping? Why someone would do it?"

"Some Hopi tea?"

"Uh. No thanks."

"The tea will calm you down."

"Calm me down?"

"Yes. You are very nervous." Izzie poured him a cup of the reddish beverage. "She has that effect on men."

"What did you say?"

She handed him a saucer. "She likes you."

Tracker laughed. "Doesn't feel like it. She's a challenge, an enigma, a little like you are."

"We Hopis are a peaceful people. We do not lie. Kate likes you. Can't you see that?"

"J.C. told me once that I didn't do well with women because I didn't know anything about them."

"Try it."

"This tea? This isn't hallucinatory, is it?"

"No. It has very special powers."

"Such as?"

In her nurse's voice, she said, "Relaxes the tissue, diminishes tension and pressure on the sensory nerves."

"Scientifically, how does it do that?"

"It dilates the capillaries, both blood and lymph. And it protects against inflammation."

Tracker held his cup out. Izzie smiled, poured more tea. "Try getting to know Kate."

∎∎∎

"Sure cools fast when the sun goes down." Tracker twirled a long spike of wild barley, absently threw it like an arrow.

"Altitude, Mr. T," said J. C. He stood, brushed off his pants, took a draw on his cigarette. "I like this spot. Near enough to the camp but far enough..." He didn't say far enough from what.

A gust of wind blew cigarette sparks in the growing darkness.

Tracker closed his eyes, but the sparks almost hurt. Hurt in a terribly sad way. He couldn't have stopped it from happening.

"What's wrong, Mr. T? You just winced, like a spider bit you or something."

"You ever think back to that night we were assigned to the Asarco Section? I can still see the fiery red slag coming down that hill from the smelter, sparks flying, hear that train coming."

"We ran as fast as we could," said J.C.

"You think she tripped, or did she commit suicide?"

"I can't let my mind go there. She had to have been Catholic. That rules out suicide. That and the baby."

They were talking about a tragic incident at the 400-acre site of ASARCO—American Smelting and Refining Company, a copper and iron smelter on a bluff a stone's throw from Mexico. A routine stakeout at a well-known spot where the river was right next to Paisano Avenue, the main drag into downtown El Paso. And directly across the Rio Grande from *La Colonia Ladrillera*, one of the poorest neighborhoods in Juárez.

■■■

A family of five—mother, father, grandmother and two tiny children, were trying to ford the river, make it to the overhead walkway, and disappear into the desert. Son wrapped securely on his back, the father turned to help the elderly woman. His wife, infant in a sling in front of her, ran ahead.

Tracker and J.C. were about a half mile away, parked in a patrol jeep, spotting the escape through binoculars. Tracker hit the gas, ripping out of the sand and mesquite bushes to swerve onto the asphalt. Smelter fires roared above them, 800-foot smokestacks contaminating central El Paso with dirty yellow smoke. The blast furnaces were emitting dangerous metals, a virtual periodic table of heavy metals: lead, arsenic, cadmium, chromium, selenium and zinc. Molten slag oozed in a semi-liquid state down the heap, sending sparks into the night sky.

A train heading west entered the curve, the engine suddenly silhouetted against the molten copper byproducts. The mother didn't see it in time. The woman was struck, going down instantly.

Tracker and J.C. jumped the guard rails, vaulted over the security fence and sprinted to the tracks. Between the roar of the furnaces, the thundering train, and heat from the slag, they were blown backwards. Tracker shielded his face, stepped back. J.C. bent over and wretched.

The engineer never saw her or her baby.

▪▪▪

"I need a drink," said Tracker.

"Capitán's close."

Tracker took off his tie, carefully rolled it. Reached into the back of the jeep, pulled on a worn denim jacket. "Any recommendation?"

"The Rusty Anchor—a former TB patient owns it."

"Join me?"

"No thanks, Mr. T. Clara's expecting me soon." J.C. rubbed his thin gold wedding band. "If I'm late, she worries. Don't have a phone."

▪▪▪

In his short drive, Tracker didn't see much population. Just a couple of miles between Capitán and Lincoln, once one of the most dangerous towns in the west. Now Lincoln was a sleepy one lane village. Most houses had electricity and running water, but there were those with kerosene lanterns, wood stoves and an outhouse. Very few telephones, like J.C. said. Rural service was slow. The only radio signals came from Juárez—okay if you like salsa and mariachi music and spoke Spanish.

All able-bodied men had gone to war. Most people in Lincoln County were flat poor. As Beaver would put it, 'flat as gravy on a plate.' Many had lost their livelihoods and property. Just like J. C. said, the bar was the first sign of life in Capitán.

Tracker passed an empty law office housed in a clean-cut territorial style building. The glass door was boarded over, painted with a sign saying, "Gone to Fight." Next door was an empty lot, full of summer grass. A deserted saddle shop, a yellowed sign in the window advertising farrier services on site.

He spotted Chávez's Garage. Permanently closed, J. C. used it as a landmark—it was directly across the street from the Rusty Anchor. The garage belonged to J. C.'s uncle, who had recently died of complications from pleurisy. His aunt was working in a line factory job in Lubbock, punching a time clock. J. C. said these days it was the only way a widowed woman could make money.

Tracker passed the bar on purpose, parking in front of The Mercantile, an original name for the one-and-only grocery/clothing/hardware store in town. The jeep would mark him as a law officer. Not the way to make new friends.

Laughter from a crowd of cowboys caught his attention. A large dark bay gelding was urinating in front of the bar. Tracker sidestepped the puddle. The windows were dirty, misted up from male bodies inside. Inside, he chose a stool at the bar. A big fan at the end of the room attempted to clear the air hanging in high-pitched trusses holding up the tin roof. Essentially a barn with a bar. He signaled the bartender, a skinny guy wearing a Hawaiian shirt.

"What'll it be, gringo?"

"A beer. Got a choice?"

"Mitchells, that's it."

"I know it; it's from El Paso." The head bubbled over the lip. Slowly pooled on the bar top. The beer was warm.

"You're lucky to have anything. Allotments are levied. Sugar's in short supply." The man was extremely pale. Long, thin fingers. Not the usual bartender type, but curious enough to say, "You're new around here."

"I work over by the fort."

"Prison camp or hospital?"

"The POW camp." Tracker introduced himself.

"I'm Cletis. Cletis Rodgers. I loved having the Krauts come in. Big beer drinkers. Pearl Harbor changed that for them." A customer in the crowded bar called for another beer.

Tracker lifted his gaze from the blue cigarette haze reflected in the mirror behind the bar to the animal heads above. Elk. Antelope. Buck deer gazed glassy-eyed. Just like the spectacle-covered eyes of President Roosevelt in a row of *Life* magazine covers tacked to a support beam. He stroked the longneck, swallowed too fast. Tried to cover up a belch.

Cletis was back.

Tracker asked, "You're a hunter?"

"Can't say I am," answered Cletis. "All those belong to the local taxidermist. He's gone to the war; he's a medic."

A customer lurched against Tracker. A calloused hand slammed an empty beer bottle on the bar top. *"Más cerveza."*

"More beer coming up."

Rugged clientele. Dry mouths gravitating to liquid refreshment. Mostly Mexican *braceros*, working summer roundups or digging up the rail beds outside of town. All available steel was being confiscated for the war effort. If they were illegals, they didn't show any fear. Tracker pulled his jacket closer, covering his uniform shirt.

"Mr. Dodds, so glad to see you." He found himself face-to-face with Stillington. "Please join me, bring your beer."

Tracker settled stiffly into a hard wood chair, stretched out his bad leg. Over loud laughter behind him, he said, "I thought it was time I meet some locals. Friendly, I discover. The bartender..."

"Cletis? He's okay. Used to be a dashing young mariner on the high seas until TB got him. Just like what happened to me."

"He looks older," said Tracker.

"He's a survivor. Hard worker. His wife, too." Stillington slowly swallowed the last measure of beer in his bottle.

"What happened to you? Did you get TB?" asked Tracker.

"I went into the Health Service in 1934. Right off the bat, they transferred me to Norfolk, Virginia. I passed to the rank of Assistant Surgeon, posted me to the Marine Hospital on Staten Island, New York. I contracted TB there. Five years later I became the Medical-Officer-in-Charge at Fort Stanton. One of my qualifications for the job was that I had had TB. Enough about me. How old are you, Tracker? I'm guessing you're thirty-eight to forty."

"Next month, fifty."

"Really?" said Stillington.

"I've been on my own a long time. Before joining the border patrol, I went on the air show circuit. Worked as a crop duster, too."

"A dangerous job, flying that low."

"I was more worried about the dust. Lead arsenate."

"My God. You really have lived dangerously. Well, young man, I am forty-five. In my prime, I'd like to think." Stillington's gaze took in the entire room. "Squandering my talent in such lovely circumstances. But then again, I could be performing surgery in a tent in the middle of a blood-soaked field in France. Let me make another assumption—you aren't overseas right now because of that leg of yours, right?"

"I couldn't pass the physical."

"Perhaps you could teach?"

"You know, that occurred to me, but I know myself better. I'd be so damn frustrated I'd die. No desk job either. I have almost enough hours for a degree. I speak Spanish fluently, grew up speaking with guys who worked for my father. I'm an expert marksman, thanks to the Corps, and I'm comfortable with strict discipline. Good at following orders, and damn good at giving orders. I've read a lot of law and criminal justice. I'm in as good a place as I can be, considering my shattered leg." Tracker took a sip of warm beer. "It seems we're both coping with handicaps."

"And what would you guess is my particular handicap?" Stillington asked, twirling the empty beer bottle on the table.

"I don't know. You're an erudite man. I would assume you would be more comfortable in a city setting. Museums, concerts, books, culture."

"I brought my books with me, my music, too. I'm afraid my path to erudition was painfully interrupted by my marriage to a beautiful woman."

"I'm not surprised," Tracker said, flashing a wry smile. "I consciously duck long term relationships."

"Are you sure about that?"

What did he mean by that? Tracker wondered.

"Surely you've noticed my lovely head nurse?"

"Miss MacAllan?"

"Yes, Tracker."

"She's a piece of work. I don't know what to think of her. She can be as feisty as a polecat. Sometimes I think she's leading me on, and then..."

"You mean she flirts with you?"

"Let's put it this way. If I could dance, I'd be afraid of dancing with her because she would lead me. Too damn pushy."

"Well, she's certainly assertive," said Stillington. "Part of being a nurse. She's extremely smart, and a perfectionist. Knows when and where to step in. In many a tight spot, I've felt comfortable letting her take over." Stillington put his hand on Tracker's shoulder. "Maybe the two of you are too much alike."

Changing the subject instead of confronting it, he asked, "Anyone in here I should meet? Anyone that could possibly help with the investigation?"

Stillington was getting to his feet, his reading glasses precariously on the edge of his nose. He didn't seem to notice. He absently stroked his goatee, lost in thought. "You might want to meet that gentleman who just came in the door. The man with the sheriff, he's the county clerk. Can I buy you another beer?"

Tracker nodded negatively. The sheriff headed straight for Dodds. No handshake. No greeting at all from Halligan or his friend. "You Feds have been out chasing escapees in my jurisdiction."

"There was a flood, sir, no time." He wanted no quarrel with the man.

"Don't 'Sir' me, Dodds." He took the bottle of beer Álvarez brought. "Be trying to soft talk me?"

"No. Just being civil."

"Civil?" Halligan drained half the bottle while looking down at Tracker. "Civility—starts with respecting your limits of authority. You can't go over my head."

"That's a crock, and you know it. I don't need to tell you a damn thing."

Tracker stood to his full height. Probably should have brought the blowhard on board, he thought. Too late for that. "Sheriff, is this your idea of cooperation?"

"You're on my turf. Goddamnit. Give me an update on the murder."

"Okay. The prisoner was, in fact, murdered. A knife wound to the belly—that's my guess."

"Not much of an investigator, are you?" No response. "Have you given thought to the possibility of an outsider?"

"Sheriff, I'll keep you informed on the progress," said Tracker.

"Damn well right you will."

"Brought you a beer," Stillington said. "Figured you might have changed your mind."

"That Halligan is a real shit head," said Tracker.

"Well said," Stillington replied. "Even on his good days."

"Why would he think Schmidt was murdered by someone outside the prison?"

"Before you came, things were handled differently. The Columbus crew were allowed to roam nearby. They had money. Remember, they weren't considered as enemies or soldiers at war when they were sent here. They bought stuff like shaving cream, soap, in the mercantile. Came in here to drink beer."

"No one tried to escape?"

"Why would they? We are so remote. The Apache Reservation surrounds us. Each road leading out of here—to Carrizozo, El Paso, or Roswell—leads to pure desert."

"Whoever picked this place was damn smart," said Tracker.

16

Mail delivery to the Fort was sporadic. The postmistress personally hand-delivered the letter to Kate just as she was leaving the hospital.

Kate studied the envelope—the paper was fine bond, with an engraved return address. Wyoming. Flipping the envelope back to the front side, she looked as if hypnotized at the red stamp marked Registered. She sprinted across the parade ground to her quarters. Her hands shook as she opened the letter and read:

JONAS HARDCASTLE
Lawyer
301 N. Grand Avenue
Laramie, Wyoming

Tel: Main 439

June 4, 1942

Dear Miss MacAllan:

May I express my deep regrets at your mother's passing, even though it is long since you and Elizabeth were in touch.

I cannot impress on you strongly enough how urgent it is that you come to Laramie as soon as humanly possible. Let me explain what makes this necessary.

Your father was a client I admired and as you know, when Daniel died in 1936 his will placed everything in Trust at First Community Bank here for your mother during her lifetime, because it was very important to him that it go to you upon Elizabeth's death without being dissipated by her while she lived, and he knew she would not leave it to you if she could avoid it. The Trust is worth approximately $1,200,000. today, including the shares in the Canadian corporations holding the mink farm and Scotch whiskey distributing company. All of the inheritance taxes were paid at the time of Daniel's death, and because the property was in a trust there are none payable now.

Now what you may not have understood in 1936 is that under Wyoming law a widow has what is called "the right of dower" in one third of the family assets, which would allow her to take that much property no matter what your father's will said. To try to keep that one third under the bank's management, Daniel's will put Elizabeth to an election, whereby she had to elect to let her dower one third go in the trust, otherwise she would not receive any benefit of the rest of the estate. To induce Elizabeth to do that, the trust gives her what we call a general power of appointment by her will over one third of the trust, under which she could appoint, that is, "give," that much of the trust to whomever she saw fit when she died.

Elizabeth's will gives everything over which she has any power of appointment to the Brethren Fundamentalist Church of Laramie. Your mother's friend and lawyer, Zeb Wilcox, has already filed it for probate and the hearing is set for June twentieth, to which the Brethren look forward, as you would expect, with gleeful antic- ipation and there will be a large crowd present. In addition I have filed the necessary court proceeding to wind up and distribute the Trust under Daniel's Will, and we can be sure Zeb and his friends will appear, smug as can be about claiming benefits under the power of appointment. I was able to have that hearing set for June twen- ty-third, two days after Elizabeth's probate hearing.

Now, Zeb is not much of a book lawyer. What they don't realize is that the power of appointment says Elizabeth may exercise it provided that she specifically refers to the power of appointment under Daniel's will, but her will does not do that. It only refers in a general way to any powers of appointment she may have, so under the Wyoming Supreme Court decision in Northcutt v. Northcutt they will be foiled completely. I must say it will be poetic justice as Charlie Norton over at the Trust Department, who is also a lawyer and a good one, told me that Elizabeth had asked him to review her will and he pointed out the defect to her several times, but each time she came in to talk about her will she got all worked up trying to figure out a way she could dispose of the entire trust, and she never got around to fixing the defect or anything else. When she had the heart attack, it spooked her. She called Zeb Wilcox, but it was too late. She died before the changes could be made.

So with that background, what makes the time so import- ant is this: George Farthing is the probate judge who will hear both of these matters, and he is an absolutely fair and honest judge who is not afraid to apply the law as it is, even if unpopular with a large number of the community. But as luck would have it, George received his draft notice this week and has to report on June 16, so the new probate judge will be Ben Johnson from over in Cheyenne, who as you know went to law school with and remained good friends of your mother and Zeb Wilcox. Ben, I am afraid, would not be able to resist trying to carry out your mother's warped wishes if he could, and we could be faced with years of appeals not to mention expense.

So do come as soon as you possibly can so we can have your signature for the necessary papers and proceed with the extensive preparation that will be necessary. If you have difficulty with wartime travel, I can certify the urgency. Awaiting your telegram letting me know the date of your arrival, I remain,

Respectfully yours,

Jonas Hardcastle
JH:jhh
Enclosures: Trust Documents, First Community Bank, Laramie, Wyoming

Folding the letter and sliding it into the envelope, Kate knew she had no time to waste or she would lose everything. But the letter had taken time making its way to New Mexico. It was the fourteenth—ten days had passed. She had twenty-four hours to get to Laramie.

17

Tracker felt a tug on the hem of his jacket. He looked down to see a young face. All eyes, like a small brown owl. The boy couldn't have been more than four years old.

"¿Señor, gusto empanadas? Empanadas de chavaconos y meil."

The boy spoke so softly he could barely hear him. Tracker leaned closer and asked to see the apricot and honey-laced pastry.

The boy averted his eyes as he spread open a cloth on the table. Tracker bought two, handing one to the doctor who was just leaving. He took a bite, asked his name. *"¿Como se llama?"*

"Paco, Paco Chávez."

"Got a problem?" asked Cletis, pointing to the boy who was already scooting out the door.

"No problem. Interesting clientele you have here."

Cletis laughed, "These men here shouldn't be spending money on beer. They should be paying off their bills at the store, buying milk for their babies. But, what the hell, they keep my doors open."

"Tell me about the little kid, Paco."

"His mother takes in laundry, gathers eggs. You'll see her hanging stuff on the clothesline before dawn. She cooks stuff and sells it on the street—she won't come in here. Someone's had their way with her, she's kind of disfigured. That's why she sends the kid. Sorry old world, isn't it?"

"I met a rancher from Hondo. He didn't look too down-and-out."

"That would be Albert Grafton," said Cletis. "Pretty slick fellow, buys up busted folks land." Cletis picked up Tracker's beer bottle, wiped the condensation from the table top. "Like a vulture. I'm not as dumb as I look. Speak a little Spanish. It's just all in the present tense. The Spaniards claimed this region in the fifteen hundreds. Mexico was established in eighteen twenty-one, and they followed the Spanish policy of making land grants. Buying land here in New Mexico is tricky. The problem is getting a clear title. That's where the shyster lawyers get involved."

"Tell me how it works," said Tracker, recalling J.C.'s info on the treaty.

"I'll give you an example. I don't know if Grafton had a stake in any of this particular deal, but these guys buying up land grants are very clever.

A guy gets title clearance for land he bought from a Mexican. This original owner, who didn't speak English, sold what he thought was four hundred hectares, that's about a thousand acres. The guy that bought it had it surveyed and it turned out to be a little over eight thousand hectares, or twenty thousand acres. In this case, they found coal. Right down the road from here. Phelps Dodge gobbled it up. The speculator made a fortune."

"Have you been in his sights?"

"Hell, yes. Tried to buy me out. Him and his partners. But I know too much."

"You pushed back?"

"Nice way of putting it."

"And you think Grafton was involved in that scheme?"

"I told you up front I didn't know if Grafton was part of it. I know I backed him down when he tried to buy me out."

•••

"How was the Rusty Anchor last night?" asked J. C.

"Beer was warm." He turned his attention back to the steno pad. He had two new entries: Halligan = asshole. Grafton = murder? Hire someone to do it?

"You got a suspect?" J. C. hunched forward in his chair, his elbow on Tracker's desk.

"Nope. Is everything in place for the funeral at eleven?"

"Yes, Mr. T."

"Double check. Boots polished. Saddles, breast collars, bridles. Especially the saddle for Beaver's boot. Everyone look their best."

•••

Kate glanced at the pencil in her hand. Teeth marks. How stupid. What a way to get TB. Tossed it into the trash. For God knows how many times, she checked the clock. Izzie was three hours late. Iz had been remote of late, irrational. Delivering wrong meds, whispering. But this was the first time she had failed to show up.

The door opened and closed softly, Kate didn't bother to look up. "And just where have you been, Miss Jahata? Late! Three goddamned hours late."

"Pardon?" asked Tracker.

Kate swiveled around. "Sorry, I thought—that Indian is driving me crazy."

Tracker watched her arch her head back, twisting her neck, fighting back tears. "I brought back your dictionary. You okay?"

"Yes, just tired."

"I was talking to Izzie, she said I should get to know you better. Are you seeing anyone?" asked Tracker.

"No. And you? Are you hiding some passionate woman in your life?"

"No. Sometimes I think I love dogs and horses more than people." He stepped around the counter and began massaging her neck.

"I couldn't agree more. Ah. That's good. Right there."

"You're tight."

"I know. I'm surprised I don't have lockjaw." She lowered her head. Her short hair shielded her eyes. "You're the strong, silent type. Didn't you ever have time for someone else?"

"I'm happy with what I'm doing."

"That's not what I asked."

"It's not like I'm anti-social. I'm just not the life of the party like you are."

She jerked her head up. "Is that a compliment? Or are you making fun of me?"

"Shhhh. Calm down. I meant you can light up a room. You're gorgeous, fun, smart. Every patient in here loves you. You make me want to..."

"What?"

He leaned down and kissed the back of her neck. "I better go before I make a fool out of myself."

He was almost out the door when she called out, "I could use more of that."

"The kiss or the back rub?"

"Both."

As he stepped outside, Izzie brushed past him as though he wasn't there.

"Get me up to date. Let's do report," Izzie said to Kate.

Kate began rattling off the status of each patient. Izzie's eyes were closed. "Are you listening to any of this or sleeping?"

"Resting my eyes."

"Ward 3, Patient A, Joseph McGee. Changed his gown and sheets twice in the night. Heavy sweats. Complete bed rest now. Cough unproductive. No sputum.

"Patient B, Robert Singer. Considerable coughing. Twice sputum showed tinges of blood. But lung sounds haven't changed.

"Patient C, James Reed. Slept through the night. Temp this A.M. normal. The laryngitis he has had is about gone."

Finally Izzie asked a question. "Any med changes?"

"No, the doctor's holding everything steady, but he wants a new round of sputum specimens today." Kate noticed that her own hands were shaking. And she knew it wasn't from low blood sugar or the vacant look on Izzie's face. She touched the spot on the back of her neck. "Take over for me, Iz."

18

Eleven o'clock. Like a silent film in sepia, three mounted patrolmen in drab green dress uniforms led the funeral procession. Flags—US, New Mexico, border patrol—hung limply at their sides. Platoon on foot behind, black ribbons over their gold badges. Tracker led a bay mare with a western style saddle. Beaver's cowboy boot and spur backwards in the left stirrup.

A jeep carried hospital staff up the muddy road to God's Acre. Locals stood respectfully in the damp grass near the freshly dug grave and flag-draped coffin. A motley scattering of mud-splattered old cars and trucks were parked outside the cemetery entrance.

When the entourage came to a halt, the men snapped a white-gloved salute. Each took a wide stance, rifle butts on the ground, parallel to their legs. Despite his sunglasses and flat-brimmed hat, Tracker cupped his left hand over his eyes, momentarily blinded by the sun.

He spotted Kate with Dr. Stillington. The doctor in his dress blue uniform and white cap, black patent brim. She was dressed in her whites. Starched cap to her stockings and shoes. Pure white. Whiter than white.

Everything else was muted, all sounds muffled. After the priest's words, "A man of color," Tracker barely heard anything. He had angina. An excruciating headache. Blood pounded, roared in his ears. He thought his bad leg was going to buckle, and put his gloved hand on the horse's breast collar for support.

He snapped rigidly to attention when the honor guard shouldered their M1 Garand rifles. The volley echoed over the vast valley. Again. And again.

That was really all he remembered afterwards.

19

Müeller looked up in surprise. The captain rarely visited the crew in their barracks. Müeller pulled back the curtain, gestured to the cots. "Reinhold, working on football field. Please sit. Something wrong with luncheon, *Kaéptin?*"

"How are your eyes?"

"Gutt, Kaéptin. Gutt." Müeller shrugged.

Daehne took a seat on the other cot. "Your knives, please. I know you keep them with you."

Müeller retrieved a leather pouch from a locked wooden box. Handed it over.

Daehne removed a stiletto-like instrument. "Used as a skewer, when cooking on the grill?"

"Ja, Herr Kaéptin."

"Speak English."

"Yes, sir."

"You've heard the talk…Klaus was stabbed to death." Daehne turned the rapier-like blade, touched his finger carefully against the sharpened steel. A chill slithered down the back of his neck. "Something like this could kill very easily, wouldn't you say?"

"Never leaves my sight."

"You seem relaxed today, Müeller. A talent I admire. One adapts to circumstance." Müeller said nothing. "Would you swear on your honor that these knives have never been left unattended?"

"Never, niné, Herr Kaéptin."

Daehne didn't admonish him for reverting to German; he was busy analyzing Müeller's body language. The always-tense, nervous cook seemed so calm, despite the line of questioning.

∎∎∎

Tracker tapped on the door frame of Stillington's office. Stillington glanced up from a file. "I've finally got something for you, Dodds, the preliminary lab report from Santa Fe. The blood studies showed Klaus Schmidt had no evidence of thrombin in his system. That's why there was no clotting." Stillington pointed to the equations in the file:

Thromboplastin Complex + Prothrombin Complex + Calcium
= Thrombin

Thrombin + Fibrinogen = Fibrin

"Meaning?" asked Tracker.

Stillington explained that thromboplastin and prothrombin were proteins in the blood, that when activated—when hemorrhaging ensues—combine to form an extremely active chemical—thrombin. Thrombin will then combine with another protein to form fibrin, the critical building block needed for blood to clot.

"So you need thrombin to have clotting—what could keep that from occurring?"

"A good question. Lots of things, but in view of the fact the bone marrow report was normal, and the blood cells in the blood were normal..." Stillington looked past Tracker, as though he were having a discussion with his mirror image, concluding the diagnosis with himself. "I remember being told once, 'If you hear horse's hooves in the street, don't think of zebras.'"

Tracker fought to control his impatience with Stillington's wandering. Focus, damnit. "Where are you going with this?"

"Ah, yes, I meant one shouldn't think of oddball things first—go with the obvious. I think the man was poisoned."

"Poisoned? You told me he was killed with an instrument that ripped up his stomach, not to mention the scalping."

"Right, Dodds. The stab wound killed him. The scalping came later. But, whoever poisoned him, then stabbed him, wanted to make absolutely sure that Klaus died. Call it an insurance policy for certain death."

"Well, this really helps." Stillington picked up the sarcasm in Tracker's voice.

"There are more tests that can be run. I've already ordered them."

"Call me the minute you get them."

He reminded himself to keep the dominos upright—this murder was well-planned. If Schmidt was poisoned, there was a time element involved, the poison needed time to work.

Tracker limped out of the hospital grateful to feel the warmth of the sun. He turned right down the parade ground walkway and saw Kate sitting alone on the back steps in the shadows of the hospital.

"What's wrong? Are you mad at me?" he asked, sitting down beside her.

She put her hand on his knee. He put his arm around her. "Not really."

"Come on, Kate, talk to me."

She faced him, her eyes filled with tears. Pulling out the lawyer's letter, she handed it to him. "When I went riding this morning, I was trying to figure out what to do. There's just no way, there's no time..."

Tracker noted the value of the estate. A fortune. He also couldn't tell Chief Vonshooven in El Paso. He made up his mind. "I'll fly you up there tomorrow."

"You'll what?" She looked skeptical,

"Get ready to leave early tomorrow. One small bag. Bring a coat, scarf, and gloves. No room for anything else."

■■■

"J. C., get in here, now, and close the door." Chávez perked up his ears. "The other day I saw a barn on top of that south mesa where the landing strip is. I didn't think much about it at the time, but the letters CPTP were painted on the side."

"Defunct Civil Pilot Training Program," said J. C.

"I thought so. By any chance is there a training plane still locked up in there?" If there wasn't a plane in that barn, he knew he was going to have to go to El Paso and 'borrow' a plane from headquarters. Fat chance of getting away with that."Yup. Saw it fly a couple times—too small for my liking. What's up?"

"Kate has a problem. She needs to get somewhere fast."

"Damsel in distress?"

"Not funny."

"Understood. Want to take a look, Mr. T?"

A trail of dust followed the jeep up the hillside. The wide double doors were chained, padlocked. Marked with a sign: No Trespassing—By Order of the Federal Aviation Authority. Before he could ask, J. C. grabbed a hammer from the toolbox in the jeep. The chain held but the door splintered. J. C. kicked it in. "It's yours, Mr. T."

A biplane. Yellow. A Jenny. Curtiss JN-4 Trainer. Surplus material. The military stopped using these babies in the twenties. Almost every U.S. airman learned to fly using this plane. He had flown one in his crop-dusting days. Forty-four-foot wing span, ten-foot length. Open air cockpit. Wings staggered in profile. Upper unit ahead of the lower.

"Take a look at the power plant."

Minutes dragged while J. C. studied the engine. "I've worked on these before. Powered by a single Curtis OX-5 series. Eight-cylinder vee-type inline piston. I can get the right tools at my uncle's garage."

"Is it in working condition?"

"The air up here is so pure and dry. Perfect for storage. Probably take me a couple hours, get the cobwebs out."

Looking at his watch, Tracker called from the jeep, "That's what you've got."

Back in his office, Tracker ended his last call. The regional office of the Civil Patrol Training Program records showed the plane in the barn was 1929 vintage, 90 horsepower, max speed about seventy-five miles per hour, endurance measured in two hours and fifteen minutes flight time.

An El Paso Patrol buddy hailed from Bell Ranch, New Mexico. Fuel would be available there—the guy's father would be watching for them. He alerted the police in Pueblo and Fort Collins, Colorado. His story—he had to pick up a runaway POW that had been caught in Wyoming. The chiefs accommodated him, though grudgingly. Both men had brothers in the service, and each of them was the 'token' sibling left home out of harm's way.

He would get the initial fuel from camp reserves. He would come up with an explanation only if his unauthorized trip was discovered by El Paso headquarters.

Pocket watch out. Clicked on tachometry indices for speed calculation. Telemetry for distances.

> Fort Stanton to Bell Ranch, 110 miles—Approx. 2 hrs.
> Bell Ranch to Pueblo, 180 miles—Approx. 2½ hrs.
> Pueblo to Fort Collins, 160 miles—About 2 hrs.
> Ft. Collins to Laramie, 65+ miles—45 - 50 min.

Ready, set.

20

"Frozen piston, one mother to fix, but it's working now," J.C. said. Together they pushed the Jenny out of the barn on to the crudely bladed runway at daybreak.

"I knew you could do it. Checklist. Cables. Struts. Tail gear." Tracker pulled his black wool cap on. Helmet, goggles. "Hey, J.C., hold this. Keep it warm for me."

Tracker pulled a wad of chewing gum from his mouth, put it in J.C.'s outstretched hand.

J.C. growled in disgust, threw it away.

"Can't believe you bit on that one," Tracker said.

Kate stepped out of the shadows. "Very funny, Tracker. Children, where do I sit?" She took the helmet Tracker handed to her. She wore riding breeches tucked into high-laced boots. Leather jacket, lined with shearling wool, white scarf at her neck. Gloved.

"In front, good view."

"Also the first part to hit the ground. I trust you, Tracker, but your leg?"

"I don't fly with my leg, silly girl. I've got a cane. Don't worry, it's like riding a bicycle. Let me check your chin strap. Up you go. There's a cup under your seat."

She reached down, found an empty peaches can.

"If you need to pee."

"What?"

"Dump it when we land."

"Damn. Macho peckerwood!" She caught his smile. "Mr. Dodds, I have gotten along so far without a dick."

J.C. patted Tracker on the shoulder, muttering, "That went well, Mr. T."

"Cover me. Don't breathe a word of this. Vonshooven can't know about anything. I'll be back before you know it."

"Like always, I got your back," said J.C.

Tracker tucked back in the cockpit, signaled J.C. to pull the wood propeller through. The engine coughed and died. Fourth try. An explosion. "Contact!" yelled J.C.

Engine alive, but rough. "Hang on," Tracker said as he started down the runway.

She gave him a thumbs up. Inwardly, she shivered with emotion. She wasn't sure it was all worth it. There was trouble waiting in Wyoming. Not to mention the enormous obligation she was feeling for the man seated behind her. She knew he was risking his job in order to help her. He never hesitated.

The first stop for fuel was a grass strip. She never thought about what comfort standing on the ground could be. It was like leaving the womb when they took off again. Time seemed not to exist. The only scenery changes were high peaks off to the left of the plane. Cold. Bone-cracking cold. Ice formed in their mouths. Teeth chattered.

Tracker broke the constant firecracker-like sound of the engine by announcing the headwaters of the Rio Grande. He was keeping an eye on the growing cloud formations. Even this early in the day he knew it was going to get even colder and rougher. Just as the thought crowded his mind, a sudden downdraft sucked at the plane; the biplane fell as though the supports were knocked out from under it. No time to think. Jammed the stick forward like he was trying to drive it into the ground.

The nose came up just in time.

Rain and lightning north of Fort Collins caused a change in the flight plan. North over Cheyenne. Weaving between towering thunderheads.

At ten-thousand feet, they were a tiny teardrop against troubled sky. The contour lines on Tracker's aeronautical charts couldn't begin to emphasize the higher relief of the terrain below. He began his descent over Big Hollow, spotting antelope galloping through the valley between the Snowy Range and Laramie Range.

Kate had to pee. Now. She awkwardly wrestled the can underneath. Let it go. Then she emptied the urine over the side, knowing some would splash back on him.

He ducked, wiped his goggles with a rag. "Okay, babe, you asked for it." He pulled the plane up into a near vertical climb. Continued around until the circle was complete, plane back in the same direction before the stunt. A 360-degree turn, except in the vertical. Upside down at the top of the loop.

Having fun. She threw him the bird with a gloved hand. Pushing her luck. She knew he was showing off and loving it. It was grand to see him enjoying himself. That is, if she didn't throw up.

Again without warning, Tracker pulled the rudder back, straight up like the loop, but kept flying up. Airspeed dropped. The aircraft fell backwards. Stalled.

Kate screamed, covered her eyes. God, he was good. She screamed again, just for effect.

Expertly, he used the rudder to rotate around its yaw axis. Until the Jenny turned 180-degrees, pointing straight down. Nose began dropping through the horizon to vertical down. Quarter loop to level flight. Gaining speed. Yawing turn, a tailside. He pulled out of the Hammerhead with a huge grin on his face.

Time to get serious. They both knew it. He turned south. Then west to Laramie. They landed at Brees Field in a downpour, skidding along a gravel strip. He cut the engine, leaned forward to touch her shoulder. "Okay?" He knew she was okay with his flying, but he sensed she was much more nervous about being in Laramie. He wanted to guard her against any pain, but he felt helpless. Her first words told him how she felt.

"The weather is appropriate," she murmured. "It's miserable."

A man in grease-stained coveralls helped Tracker block and tie down the biplane. The oval patch on his chest read: Cowboy Aviation, followed by the name, Earl. Earl didn't waste any time telling them he didn't have any fuel to sell. Tracker said he didn't need any—he had more than half a tank remaining. Earl said he could get them the three miles into town. The airfield appeared deserted—only one derelict bi-wing was tethered down. Earl appeared to be a little bit of everything—mechanic, field manager, transportation provider, an important person to have on your side. He also let Kate use the telephone to call a much-relieved Jonas Hardcastle. The hearing was set for nine o'clock the next morning. He would meet her at his office at eight, fill her in. They could walk across the street to the courthouse.

"Have you met this man, Kate?" asked Tracker.

"I think so. A long time ago. I was just a kid. Maybe I'll place him when I see his face."

They went straight to Kate's mother's house, passing along Laramie's main street, Grand Avenue, and the Brethren Fundamentalist Church. Earl's old Pontiac, much of the gray paint rusted away, pulled into the driveway.

"Here you are, Miss MacAllan," said Earl. "My condolences."

Kate stepped from the car and looked at the home she hadn't seen for years. A black wreath hung on the front door. The two-story red brick walls once covered with ivy were bare, bits of dead branches and roots clung to the mortar like dead centipedes. The steps were in need of paint. She tentatively reached for the tarnished brass knob. The door opened, exposing the black-and-white marble-tiled floor. Cold tile.

"I'll wait out here," said Tracker.

"No, please, I need you."

He saw the shadow seconds before she did, signaled her with his index finger to his lips. In a whisper, he said, "Back door." She nodded. He disappeared inside, quickly and quietly.

The electricity had been cut off. The house was dank, cold. Floors littered with dead moths, mouse droppings. Practically no furniture. A box half-filled with books. Framed family photographs knocked over on a shelf. Some with broken glass. He made a guess, entered a room past the staircase.

"What do you think you're doing?" Tracker roared. "Get out of here!"

Feet from the rear entrance, Kate heard his booming voice. Tracker yelled again even louder. A clay pot filled with a dead geranium crashed through the screen door. A hunched figure, dark hat pulled down, flew out the door, stumbled, dropped a box of dishes, and fled. Round saucers went rolling through the thick, uncut grass. A tea cup rolled between her boots.

Later on, she realized she had never heard him raise his voice before.

She joined him in the kitchen. Once they were sure the rest of the house was empty, she mentally took inventory of what was missing. Grandfather's rocking chair, her father's leather wingback. Gone. Glass bookcases, grand piano, too. Her father's roll-top desk had disappeared. Tears streamed down her cheeks as she climbed the staircase to the bedrooms. Not one piece of furniture in any of the four bedrooms. She opened the master closet. Fur coats gone.

Tracker waited downstairs. "Did you see his face?" she asked.

"No. I got close enough to knock that pot against his head. Looks like he was working on the kitchen. Most cabinets are empty. Jesus, Kate, even the canned goods are gone."

"I didn't deserve this," Kate said with a weary sigh. "But honestly, I'm not surprised. These people sure don't have any sense of decency."

"My Mother squandered things, always wanted more. She was obsessed with square footage, having the biggest house in town. What a waste of time and money."

"What pisses me off is these people made a conscious choice," said Tracker.

"It would be an understatement to say they certainly have mislaid their moral compass."

21

They made a quick dash in the drizzle. Tracker registered them at the Medicine Bow Hotel. Though they were long sitting in the dining room, both their plates were virtually untouched.

"We're in beef country, I expected it to be better," Tracker said. "Not grain fed."

"I guess we should be glad we could even get some," Kate replied, looking past him at a table of grey-bearded ranchers and their equally aged cowhands. They were wearing their city finery, white shirts, black silk scarves. Branding time was the big subject—with no young men available, they had a lot of work ahead. So did Kate.

He ordered a bottle of blackberry wine, something to relax her, he thought. A bit sweet, but the bottle was nearly empty.

"Another bottle?" Tracker asked, knowing that neither of them were the least bit relaxed.

"Only if we can have it in my room." She quickly added, "I'm really tired, I'd like to get away from all this commotion."

They ascended the staircase slowly, heads down, assumingly concentrating on the worn, absurdly busy pattern in the carpet. The key, on a long wooden tag, dangled from her hand. She handed it to him. There was something about the way she gave it to him that caused a lump in his throat. He swallowed, inserted the key, opened the door. The sound of the chambers turning in the lock seemed very loud. He poured the wine, sat down on a straight back chair. She leaned against the headboard.

They talked about everything, from the Victorian portrait of a wall-eyed girl in the lobby to the old cowboy with as many whiskers in his ears as his drooping moustache. Nothing of consequence. He emptied the last of the wine into her glass.

"Yours is empty, help me finish mine," she said, holding out her glass. He sat beside her. Took a small sip. Kate took his hand. "You've done all you possibly could to help me out." She intertwined her fingers with his. "You're actually much nicer than you act—you are quite intimidating, Tracker."

"Is that why you threw piss at me?"

She laughed. "Luckily, most of it missed you."

"Not all of it. I deserved it. You can be so feisty."

"You have no idea just how feisty I can be." It was raining hard, sheeting the window.

She liked the feel of his chest against her, his smell. She pushed him back, slowly unbuttoned his shirt. He watched her intently as she pulled his khaki shirt loose.

Naked, they slid between the cool sheets, their hands exploring each other. No words.

Tracker slipped out from the sheets and into his clothes. He leaned over and kissed Kate on her cheek, then his lips found hers. He closed the door to her room having not said a word.

Kate was gone when he went downstairs for breakfast. Over his coffee, his mind kept turning back to the day before and the cold tiled foyer at the MacAllan house.

"Good morning," said Kate, bending to lick, then kiss the back of his neck. She was dressed in a black suit, narrow skirt, short, fitted jacket with padded shoulders. A red flared-collar silk blouse. Red lipstick and nails. High heels. A slouchy, if not sexy, black hat. "Good morning, handsome. I needed lipstick. Found a drugstore close by. How's my pilot?"

"Great. Just planning the trip back." He moved his battered chart bag to the floor. Dropped his leather bomber jacket on top. Tapped the chair next to him.

Kate sat down, obviously on edge. "I called Mr. Hardcastle, got directions to his office. The Brethren are licking their lips, but he thinks he's got them by the balls."

"His words or yours?"

"His. He sounds like a real character. But my father chose him. He said he might need me here for another couple of days. What would that do to your timing?"

"I'll wait." Tracker's job was in limbo. Or worse. "I'm not going anywhere."

"I know how much I need you, but you've done more than enough."

"Don't like my flying?"

"I love your flying." She leaned closer to him. "Tracker, this whole thing. Hits close to the bone. Because of my mother, memories. It wasn't that she was strict; she was mean. I don't think she should have had a child. She was so intelligent, and she adored my father, but she never showed any love for me."

"Maybe she was jealous of you."

"It was more than that. I've had the same nightmare more than once. I open the front door and there's a rock wall almost to the ceiling. The top is covered with pieces of broken glass shards. Green, brown, blue—sharp, and..."

Tracker pulled her close, wrapping his arms around her. A waitress backed away. "It was a dream. A very visual dream."

She fingered a button on his shirt. "Freud would've loved it." She pulled her jacket closer, as if she felt a chill. Face pale. "Forgive me in advance. I may resort to wrapping a shield around myself."

"I'll be right at your side."

"What if I really do inherit everything? I'm so afraid. I don't have a long range plan."

"You have me." He saw that she was on the verge of crying. "Kate, if anything is lacking in you, it certainly isn't lack of backbone. You have too much backbone."

"Will it change me? The money?"

"Not in the way you think." He tightened his black tie, checked his pocket watch. "We'd better be going." He paid the check, left a big tip. Leaning over with the support of his cane, he scooped up his chart bag and jacket.

Kate hesitated as they walked through the lobby. "You don't ever talk about your parents. Are they deceased?"

"I left when I was sixteen. I'll tell you sometime. Let's take care of you now."

22

They had to wait a few minutes. Mr. Hardcastle was on the phone, and though there was a paneled wall and closed door between them, they could hear his voice loud and clear. Heavy footsteps, the door flung open, and a booming welcome. "Miss Kate! A pleasure to see you again. You were just a little woggin when Sally and I last saw you. I have to say you have blossomed. And your friend?" Hardcastle gestured to Tracker.

"Dodds. I'm a friend. Tracker Dodds."

Hardcastle reached out to shake his hand. Luckily, Tracker raised his bandaged hand in time to stop him. Hardcastle spotted the cane, too. "A long story. We can explain later," said Tracker.

They sat together in straight-back chairs, facing an impressive desk. Double-breasted jacket wide open, cufflinks gleaming, Hardcastle paced, smoked, ran a hand through his thick white hair. He stopped, leaned forward on his desk, vest buttons almost popping. "Kate, I don't want to be blowing sunshine up your skirt. Things can go wrong. No horn tooting this early. But these SOB's are licking their lips and wanting their cake now. Your cake! They're sitting there, drinking their sweet lemonade spiked with moonshine, just waiting to eat you up." He slammed the desk with a fist. "But we're going to whip their asses. Sanctimonious shitheads. This is going to be fun." A hand through his hair again. Lit another cigarette. "When it's over, we'll come back here to celebrate, and you'll have to sign a stack of papers. Then you can be on your way back to New Mexico, that is, unless you want my Sally to whip up one of her special dinners tonight."

"Thank you, Jonas. We've both got an awful lot on our plates back home. "Tracker flew me up here, so we..."

"He flew you up here?" Hardcastle's voice went up an octave. "Hot damn! Dropped my cracker in the chili. Sure wish you had more time." A secretary knocked at the doorway, pointed to her watch. Hardcastle nodded, began buttoning his jacket. He checked his hair in the mirror, started to pocket the cigarettes, but didn't.

Setting a brisk pace, he said, "While we walk, tell me all about your plane. Where you learned to fly. Are you good? What would I have to do to get a ride? Hot damn! This is going to be fun."

■■■

Jonas Hardcastle did his job. Stymied all moves by Zed Wilcox. Judge Ben Johnson ruled in Kate's favor. The Brethren Fundamentalist Church members present in the courtroom sat in silence, watching their anticipated windfall evaporate. All they had was the ill-gotten booty taken from Elizabeth MacAllan's home.

It all transpired in two hours. Hardcastle escorted her back to his office. It was over. Kate was leaving Wyoming a very wealthy woman.

Tracker excused himself, headed for the airport. Earl was waiting with the current weather data. The Jenny was ready and waiting. He looked at his watch. No time to waste. They could be back at dusk if all went okay.

Jonas drove her to Brees Field, straight on to the tarmac. Kate had changed clothes at the attorney's office. A secretary had packed sandwiches, a thermos of coffee.

A handshake, a kiss on his cheek, and she was in her seat. Earl gave the propeller a spin, and two-thumbs-up to Tracker.

Hardcastle and the mechanic watched the bi-plane taxi away, lift, then circle back and dip a wing. Kate waved. The plane disappeared to the south.

She watched Colorado slip past. The wicked witch was dead—that one fact consumed all her thoughts. Yet, a sense of grief, including guilt, gnawed at her conscience. She would find a way to forget her mother, her childhood. With the help of the man behind her. It was extremely cold, but smooth. She finally let it go and fell asleep.

Eight hours and a fuel stop later, they approached the landing strip. He had worried about the light, had even planned to land earlier and wait for morning. He shifted stiffly.

A rainbow of light struck the windshield, refracting on a chrome fitting. An instant before the vivid pink light disappeared, the high alpine peak of Sierra Blanca shone like emerald green velvet. The flash of light was gone as quickly as it had come. The sunset began to fade. They descended in near darkness, landing in ambient light.

He checked the luminous face of his pocket chronograph. In less than twenty minutes he would salute the guard and hit the ground running. Three days left. He had never heard of the Provost Marshall General. Neither had J.C., who later told him Major General Allen Gullion currently headed the Army branch in charge of all foreign incarceration in the US during wartime. An institution established in 1776, with great responsibility. No wonder Vonshooven had levied a deadline. Focus, man, focus.

He taxied toward the barn at the end of the field. A black sedan with interior lights on was parked next to the jeep. 'Sheriff' was clearly scripted in white on the doors.

"Oh, shit."

Tracker killed the engine, the blades spun. Silence. Halligan sat motionless in his car, hat pulled down over his eyes, presumably asleep. Tracker and Kate watched him for several minutes before he helped her to the ground. They swung the wooden tail skid around, pushed it into the hanger. They were closing the large doors when the sheriff finally got out of the sedan.

"Been waiting long?" asked Tracker.

"You might say that. Even called El Paso to see if you'd headed down there." Halligan tucked his thumbs in his belt.

"Family emergency." Tracker wasn't giving up any more, the sheriff was playing with him.

Kate smiled sweetly at the sheriff and slipped into the jeep. Tracker turned the ignition. Nothing. Another grinding crank which slowly screeched to nothing. Tracker swallowed a curse.

"Dead battery? Well, I'll be—come on, I'll give you a lift back to the hospital." By the look of the grin on his fleshy face, turkey gobbler hanging over a yellowed collar, Halligan still had a good bit more to say. "Your Chief wants to talk to you."

Tracker opened the back door of the dusty black car. Kate touched his hand as she slid into the backseat.

Tracker was tired. Very tired. As they pulled away in the darkness, he inhaled and blew out his words to the sheriff. "Did Chief Vonshooven tell you that I informed the Civil Air Patrol of my flight plans? As a Federal officer, and especially when we are at war, it is my duty to take action in the face of an emergency."

"Well, your girlfriend there was sorely missed. You might be interested," Halligan said, pointing to a fresh mound barely visible in the cemetery near the fence. "No cross yet.""Who is it?"

"Her patient, Philip Anderson." Halligan glanced back at Kate. "Doc Stillington was unavailable and your nurse friend was nowhere to be found. You both ought to show more respect for people, for the law. Only stupid people screw up. I thought you were smarter than that." He slowed, pulled in front of the lighted guard house at the Marine Hospital. Stopped.

Tracker opened the door and was instantly out, Kate right behind him.

"Drive you to the POW camp, Dodds?" The light inside the car emphasized the broken blood vessels in Halligan's cheeks and nose.

"No. I'd rather walk."

"Inspector Dodds, I'm going to have your ass. You broke the law. You stole that plane."

■■■

Tracker went straight to his office. Ignored a snappy salute from the agent on the radio. Slammed the door. A knock broke the silence. "Who is it?"

"Mr. T," said J. C. "You're back."

"That's obvious. Fill me in."

Rata-tat-tat, J.C. admitted things had gotten a little out of hand while Mr. T was gone. The sheriff demanded permission to interrogate some of the prisoners. J. C. agreed only after Halligan threatened to call El Paso headquarters, tell them no one was in charge, and that, in fact, SPI Dodds was nowhere to be found and was openly stealing fuel for a stolen plane to take his lady friend for a joy ride.

"Halligan threatened to call Chief Vonshooven, but didn't?" asked Tracker.

"That's right," said J.C.

"Who was questioned?"

"The guys who work in the stables."

"Any of them that I know specifically?"

"Klaus Schmidt worked there. Schmidt made regular trips into Capitán on a back route. Other crew men covered for him. No one would talk."

"I'm going into Capitán. Get some men up to my jeep. Battery's dead. You damn well had better keep a tight lid on this place. It leaks info like a sieve, and it seems a prisoner can come and go at his pleasure."

"Whoa, Mr. T. That was before we got into the war. Look, I lied for you to that stinking fat sherriff."

"You saved my career," said Tracker wearily.

"Saved on paperwork," said J.C. "Almost forgot, before you go, take a look at what came in the pouch today. It's addressed to both of us." The envelope held a week-old clipping from the *El Paso Times.* A note was paper-clipped to it, saying, 'Pretty good work for two rookies.' Signed, Chief Robert Vonshooven.

JUÁREZ DRUG BOSS LISA BARRAGÁN ARRESTED

The Chihuahua State Attorney General, in cooperation with the FBI and Border patrol from the El Paso Sector, have agreed to the arrest and extradition of Juárez drug capo Lisa Barragán to the United States. She is accused of running the drug trade, including opium, morphine and cocaine, planning and carrying out the murders of eleven Chinese immigrants dedicated to the sale of narcotics.

"She was the brains of the operation, and the leader of herding her drug gang," said Texas Attorney General Don Fuentes. Fuentes pointed out there wasn't an industrial base big enough in El Paso or San Antonio to justify the filled-to-the-brim status of their Federal Reserve Bank branches, which he determined were full of money being laundered by narcotraffickers.

"Well, I'll be damned," said Tracker. "We were lucky to get out of Juárez, much less with that watch. That's a big score for the border patrol. Makes that debriefing we had to go through worth it."

"You were the one who remembered every detail."

"And now we're in trouble again. About seventy-two hours left to solve the murder, or I'm behind a desk forever."

∎∎∎

"Cletis, a cold Mitchell this time. None of that warm camel piss. Place is quiet tonight."

"It's late."

"Got anything to eat?" Tracker asked.

"Half a ham sandwich."

"I'll take it." He wondered if Kate was getting something to eat. How was she? She must be taking Anderson's death damn hard. He would ask her first thing next morning. Going to be a cold bed tonight. Would she be thinking the same thing?

Tracker noticed a framed photo tucked behind a liquor bottle on the shelf behind Cletis. Two rows of tuberculosis patients. Seated men, some in wheelchairs in the front row. None of them looked healthy, especially the one in the middle.

Cletis pushed a plate toward him, caught his glance, handed the photo to Tracker. "That's me on the end, in a wheelchair, in front of the therapy building. That's my future wife, Mary, in the back row. I'm a lunger." He blew his nose. "These four in the middle are dead. The black-haired fellow here, too."

"You have a hint of an accent—Boston?"

"Close. Maine. From a family of lobstermen. I enlisted in the Merchant Marine, me and five brothers."

"You didn't go back east after you recovered?"

"Thanks to Mary." Cletis laughed. "She can be mighty persuasive. She was born in Aruba, Netherland Antilles. Can't stand the cold—the Maine kinda cold."

"Smart woman. Any good loose talk lately?"

"Don't pay attention. Not interested. I do know you and that pretty nurse high-tailed it out of here in a plane a day or two ago."

"Miss MacAllan," said Tracker.

"Haven't had the pleasure of meeting her, but my wife knows her." Cletis fished for a glass in the murky wash bowl. "Mary works in the laundry at the Fort. Said she was a lovely woman."

"That she is."

What Cletis didn't mention to Tracker was what his very shaken wife had told him about Nurse MacAllan. Mary had taken a lunch break, gone out the back door of the steam laundry. The laundry crew had planted a substantial vegetable garden; she was in hopes of a fresh tomato. Then she saw her, almost stumbled over her.

Mary had barely recognized her as the Head Nurse. Kate's hair was plastered with pig manure, straw, mud. Blouse torn, neck bruised. The metal rivet button on the fly of her Levi waistband was torn off. Despite being wedged against the partially open door to the boiler room, the woman's teeth were chattering, her eyes wild.

Mary had sheltered the poor woman with her own ample body, taking her inside to a small bathroom to bathe and dress her. Kate had begged her not to tell a soul.

Listen, Cletis," said Tracker, changing the subject. "You said the Germans used to come around, right?"

"Until you guys stopped them after Pearl Harbor got hit."

"You recall Klaus Schmidt? From the *Columbus* crew?"

"Maybe. Last time you were here you wanted to know all about Albert Grafton."

"Did I?"

"Yeah. About how he bought out the down-and-out ranchers around here. Well..." He paused for emphasis. His face flushed. Even the mention of the name, after what Grafton had done to his wife, infuriated him. The glass slipped to the floor. He didn't seem to notice.

Tracker locked eyes with him.

"I despise him. He insulted my Mary. Tried to hire her to work at his ranch after Paco's mother got hurt. She turned him down. The bastard called my Mary a Dutch charwoman. She had to hogtie me to stop me from killing him. That foreman of his is another story."

"Paul Chino?"

"Yep. Grafton fathered him."

Interesting, Tracker thought. Why didn't Grafton claim his own son? Give him his name?

Reading his thoughts, Cletis said quietly, "Paul's a half-breed. If the tribe knew the truth, he'd be an outcast."

"And this way, Paul can move back and forth between the two societies."

"Right," said Cletis.

Tracker made a mental note. Paul Chino is a man who cannot only cross boundaries, he knows where the boundaries are.

23

Kate had promised Izzie she would cover her for 24 hours—she owed her that much. She changed into her uniform, quickly crossed the parade ground in darkness. She checked wards and private rooms. Izzie was nowhere to be seen. A metal door banged loudly in the stairwell, echoing through the quiet, semi-darkened hospital. Too quiet.

She trotted upstairs to Dr. Stillington's office. The door was ajar. She smelled liquor. Stillington had a glass to his lips, a bottle on the desk. He almost knocked it over when he set the glass down.

Unable to control herself, she said, "Why?" Stillington shrugged. Which infuriated her. "Why do you drink? You're a brilliant doctor!"

"None of your business. Welcome back, my dear Kate."

"It is my business, Doctor. I've watched too many near mistakes."

"Not true—I'm good, damn good."

"That you are, but you could be so much better."

"You should have knocked," Stillington said softly. His fingertips tapped a yellow piece of paper. He pushed the telegram toward her.

"Bad news?"

Stillington's eyes looked like black holes. He stood up behind his desk, lamp light from the green-glass shade reflected on his glasses. He gently touched the pull-chain switch, watched the brass chain swing back and forth. He poured another drink, stepped back, butting against the window sill. He steadied himself, took a sip. The blinds were partially open to the black night. He spoke slowly. Sadly. "My ex-wife is dead."

He told her that he met his wife while in medical school at Tulane. Ella Jane Boudreau was a real looker, a southern belle, complete with her daddy's money.

Ella was a porcelain-skinned beauty, dark brunette, an hourglass figure. She wore her hair just like her mother, in a chignon. Very New Orleans upper crust. He met her in his third year of medical school. Married the day after he graduated. Somehow he obtained a rare and prestigious appointment as a resident at Tulane Hospital. A month later, they were moved into a lovely antebellum home just off St. Charles Avenue, a wedding present from her parents.

Ella's mother took root. By the third year of his residency, things really came apart. After pulling a 36 hour stint, he found Ella and her mother sipping their way through a second bottle of Spanish extra-dry. Neither noticed him. He walked over to a silver butler tray, poured himself a drink, took the bottle of Scotch upstairs.

Kate felt like she was watching a gentle, brilliant man literally gut himself.

"I'm sure you're wondering about our love life. Turns out the belle was frigid."

Stillington sat down. "That night, I was finishing off the bottle when Ella walked in. I think she enjoyed what she said to me that night. Called me a drunk."

She told him what he had long expected, that her daddy had given $100,000 to the medical school, buying Stillington's residency.

"I told her it wasn't a world of perception she lived in. It was pure deception."

She slapped him. Told him to get out.

Kate stepped back and left, closing the door to Stillington's office very quietly.

Kate cringed. Stillington's story hurt. A brilliant man had been humiliated. He had taken on a career that put him hidden in the fourth largest state in the country. He never whined about the isolation because he wanted it, needed it. Just like she herself had done.

Stillington had just come on board at the Marine Hospital when Kate assumed her assignment. He, in fact, had promoted her to Chief Nurse a few months later. Stillington was heavily involved in the re-purposing of the Fort as a TB hospital, supervising the remodel and enlargement of the facilities, bringing in the latest medical equipment available in 1939. The research and planning, not to mention the expense, had taught Kate a lot more about property management. If only she could manage her new wealth as wisely.

■■■

Paul waited until he saw Tracker leave, then slipped out of the Rusty Anchor and on to his horse. As usual, no one even knew he had been there. Earlier in the evening, Sheriff Halligan had been mouthing off to a bunch of regulars, including a very drunk county clerk. Paul heard enough—his boss was in the sheriff's sights. Halligan's interest was tweaked enough to go after what he called that 'land-grabbing Grafton.'

At the outskirts of town, Paul urged the horse into a gallop and headed toward the Hondo Valley.

24

Daybreak was chilly for June, the air crisp. Miles downriver in a secluded opening, Izzie, in full paint, knelt beside a small fire. Softly chanting. The light breeze carried the rhythmic lyrics to Paul's ears. A ceremony to cleanse and heal. To wash away bad influences from her body. She was preparing the area for prayer, keeping bad spirits from entering so she could make peace with her gods for the death of her lover.

The cave where it all happened was six miles away.

■■■

The first words out of Tracker's mouth were, "Let's have a chat with Müeller." Tracker put on his dark glasses, reached for his hat.

"Good morning to you, too," said J.C. "Why bother with him? Like you always say, go to the top, let's go after Captain Daehne."

"No. Officers keep themselves elevated way above their subordinates. Especially these German officers. They like dealing with graphs, charts, numbers, not reality. I doubt he really knew what Schmidt even looked like. I mean it."

"Why the stables?" asked Müeller.

J. C. answered Müeller with a nightstick jabbed between the shoulder blades.

"We both know you know one helluva lot more than you're saying," said Tracker. "Maybe you will loosen up away from the safety of your little hole in the kitchen."

"I cook, that's all."

Müeller was showing unexpected defiance, Tracker thought. Where was the man getting such spunk? "Remember how you claim to have been Schmidt's friend? This was where he worked, right?"

Müeller kicked at the dirt, he was cornered, trapped like the horses in the corral. "*Jah*, he took care of horses, that's how he ride so much."

"To Capitán?" asked Tracker. Müeller was stubborn. Towering over him, Tracker placed a hand on Mueller's shoulder, pressure-pushing his thumb into the man's chest just below the clavicle. "Enough of your shit, Müeller, you damn well know exactly what was going on!"

Müeller jerked away, but Tracker forced his face toward him. "Are you a part of the money?"

"Klaus make money, not me."

"I don't believe you."

"I never took money."

"I thought you were his best friend?"

Müeller shook his head. "No. He bought me. I was his. I belong to him."

"What all did you do for him? Pimp for him?" This time Müeller nodded affirmatively. "Did he beat these women?"

"One. Maria. She had little boy, made him watch while he carved initial in her cheek."

Tracker connected. The little four-year-old boy selling pastries in the bar.

Paco Chávez.

He grabbed the man by the neck in a chokehold. Müeller's face nearly exploded. A horse whinnied nervously, reared back, striking another. The rest of the herd skittered away.

"You knew he was vicious. How could you work for someone like that, accept his money? You are disgusting!" Müeller's knees buckled. He lay motionless in the dirt. "Come on, you little bastard, talk! I swear, I'll bust your balls if you don't start talking! Give me the stick, J. C."

"Stop, please...stop," Müeller choked, his words a bare whisper. "I had to..."

Tracker kicked a clod of horse manure at his mouth, then stepped firmly on Müeller's wrist. A breathy torrent of words spilled forth.

Müeller told them he had received word that his father had lost his job; the family had been forced to send his sister to work for the Schmidt family. The girl was in bondage, both physically and sexually. Klaus's mother was particularly brutal. A bizarre, sick German *ménage a trois.* The money he made from Klaus bought his sister's freedom.

"Rich, spoiled America." His lip quivered, blood-streaked saliva dripped to his shirt. "My ship dock in New York. Bright lights, fancy cars, ladies in fur, no fear, no air raids."

The outburst didn't faze Tracker. He smelled raw vengeance in the man, "Leg irons. Solitary, no water, no shit bucket."

J. C. hefted the German to his knees, Tracker prodded Müeller's

Adam's apple with the stick. "Were you there when Schmidt cut the 'S' in Maria's face?"

"I hold her down."

Tracker wanted to break his neck. J.C. slowly spread Tracker's fingers and touched the nightstick. Tracker dropped it in the straw.

●●●

J.C. figured Tracker was in such a bad mood, more bad news couldn't make the day any worse. He opened the door at headquarters, held it for Tracker. "Want some of that special tea?"

"Good idea. I need something to calm me down."

As if an afterthought, he said, "Hey, Mr. T. Almost forgot to tell you. Nothing wrong with your battery."

"What?"

"I found a potato stuffed up the tail pile. Real tight fit. Exhaust couldn't exit the cylinder so the engine couldn't run."

"A fucking potato? I could poke a potato up Halligan's fat ass! Bring me the bottle of tequila!"

J.C. poured two glasses. Tracker downed his in one gulp.

"¿Más?"

"Por favor," said Tracker. "How's your sleep been lately, J.C.?"

"With a two-year-old?"

"At least you have a good reason. Every time I close my eyes, I'm in the flood, I see Beaver's face."

"Was that the first time you've seen a flood?"

"No. When I lived in Colorado. Beautiful countryside, except when there's a downpour. I've seen houses, wagons, livestock washed away."

"Me, too," said J.C. "Once I was staying with my uncle in Capitán. A big rain hit. There's a low spot where a homeless family was camping. Two of them were swept away. My uncle tried to help, everyone in town did, but you can't believe the power of the water."

Another sip of tequila. Tracker put the cork in. "Do you ever think bad things are justified?"

"Well, sometimes. When a soldier kills an enemy. That's justified." J.C. rubbed the back of his neck. "Yes, Mr. T, some things are meant to be."

●●●

"What? Say that again. What did you hear?" Grafton said.

In a quiet measured voice, Paul told him that Halligan was going to prove Grafton stole land around the state. "Somehow he knows about the titles."

"How?" asked Grafton. "That sonofabitch is scared of no one, besides he doesn't have the brains of a soda cracker. He doesn't know shit about Land Grants. The Spaniards were as smart as Alexander. Give'em land. The ultimate gift. Placate the Spanish officers. Placate the Pueblos by enforcing the Four Square League Law by giving each Indian pueblo an allotment of one league in each direction. No grant could cover the land. Guaranteed boundaries, cultures." Grafton was almost shouting. "Brilliant. A buffer zone between the Indian tribes."

"I know the names of every leading family who profited from the Spanish hierarchy—Los Griegos, Los Montoyas, Los Poblanos, the Armijo family, Los Gallegos—on and on. No one spoke English, so to confirm their grants, they needed a lawyer, one that was fluent and knew the ins-and-outs of the Surveyor General's office. It was so screwed up. Like slicing up a pie."

He was in a position to straighten out the validity of land grant claims. Couldn't always find boundaries. Some grants overlapped. Owners lost their original papers. The Court of Private Land Claims ruled on grants totaling 34.6 million acres, and he had dealt with hundreds of them. With a gesture of self-absolution, Grafton said, "When they couldn't pay me, I accepted land as payment. You've heard me say that before, but now I'm going to show you something you don't know about."

He took a small box from his desk drawer. Inlaid with different shades of wood. His hands were fast. Manipulating the sides of the box, a corner wedge slipped outward. Another shift. The other side moved, then the entire bottom slid back to reveal a small key.

He inserted the key just inside an eye-level bookshelf. Pushed. Not much pressure. The door of bookshelves opened to reveal an eight-by-ten storage room. Two sides lined with cubbyholes holding tubes.

A large faded map of New Mexico was tacked to the third wall. The legend read:

LAND GRANTS, 1689–1853
(1-20) SPANISH INDIAN PUEBLO GRANTS
(21-88) SPANISH GRANTS (1650–1799)

(89-106) SPANISH GRANTS (1800–1821)
(107-116) MEXICAN GRANTS (1821–1829)
(117-141) MEXICAN GRANTS (1830–1853)

∎Small land grant
∎∎Large land grant

Paul hadn't said a word.

"See the areas I've marked in pink?" Grafton asked. Paul nodded. "They're mine." He pointed to both side walls. "Here are the titles. Clear titles. And they will be yours someday. I am the largest land owner in the State of New Mexico."

For a moment back in the office, Paul's chapped, weathered face reddened. But it wasn't from embarrassment. He spoke. "I believe the land belongs to all. I see no crime involved."

"Interesting POV," said Grafton, sliding the last part of the puzzle box shut. He moved slowly to a leather couch, saying, "At least Schmidt is out of the way."

"Müeller's just as dangerous," said Paul.

"That little guy? Hell, that Klaus was a bad man, pure evil, no morals, a liar, vindictive bastard. He would stop at nothing—just as soon cut my eyeballs out and eat'm for dinner. Ah, makes me sick about that maid." Grafton's voice was low and terse. "Did you know that he tortured Maria to get that key?"

Like a striker hitting a flint stone, Paul said, "Yes, I knew it. Be careful. Müeller wants everything you have and more. Just like Schmidt."

∎∎∎

Curfew. Lights out in the prisoner's quarters. Tracker announced he was taking a walk. Approaching the new bridge across the Bonito, he heard a 'swacking' sound followed by a splash of water. A man in a white lab coat over an argyle vest and knickers was trying to tee up a golf ball. He was having trouble placing it on the ever-so-slim tee.

Stillington. Tracker watched the very inebriated doctor whiff his next swing. His golf shoe spikes were the only thing keeping the man upright. Then Tracker spotted the Buck knife stuck in the ground next to a faded khaki golf bag. He backtracked, waded across the slowly bubbling river, coming up the bank right behind the golfer. Stillington was on his knees, hands gripping the knife, blade facing him, tip touching his lab coat. And his belly.

Tracker leapt. Kicked the knife. Stillington was thrown backwards. With one hand, Tracker closed the knife, slipped it in his pocket.

Stillington pushed his glasses in place, rubbed his right hand. Then took a sip from a pint laying in the grass. Bacardi rum. Tracker reached down, picked up the open bottle of Coke, passed it to him.

"Celebrating?" asked Tracker.

"No. Drowning my sorrows. Falling on my sword, so to speak. While you're serving, pass it to me handle first."

"No. The Buck stays with me." Tracker put his hands under Stillington's arms, raised him to a standing position. Placed his arm around the shorter man's shoulders.

"Let me go," said Stillington.

"Can't leave you alone. No blame on you."

"Drunk. No good."

"Not true. Weight of the world is on you."

"Two men died yesterday. Death rate—unbearable."

"You take the worst TB cases in the country. Kate told me."

"No one will miss me."

"Are you good at golf?" Tracker asked.

"Was. I was underestimated at sports. Pretty coordinated. Could hold my liquor." The doctor wiped his nose indignantly. "You know what I mean?"

"Wager? You and me. The longest drive," said Tracker. Stillington laughed, shook his head. "Thought not. Let's go home. Coffee, do you have any?"

"No."

"Izzie has tea, great tea." The hospital alarm sounded. Low at first. Louder, and sustained.

Code Zero.

"Tracker, I must go. It's okay, I'm okay." His voice was clear, no unsteadiness. "Really. I'm only happy when I work. My axons haven't been functioning properly. You know, the connectors between cells in the brain." He set off at a trot toward the hospital. Stopped and called back to Tracker. "Would you mind keeping my things for a while?

25

Two days left. Between the encounter with the damn cook, and worry over Stillington's attempt to commit *hari-kari*, he couldn't keep his eyes shut. He got up, locked the doctor's knife in the gun case, leaned the golf bag up in the corner of his office. Poor Mrs. Chávez, Paco's mother, disfigured for life. It made him sick. The sheriff hadn't done a thing about it.

He looked at the notes he'd made sometime during the night, ripped them out of the notepad and stuck them in his shirt pocket. The page contained a list, the order dictated by probability.

Müeller was at the top. Grafton next, the greedy bastard. Izzie was a question mark. She could be the scalper, she would know how to do it, but he doubted she was capable. Then there was Paul Chino, impenetrable, and dedicated to Grafton.

He ordered his horse saddled. The Appaloosa made his own way through a clump of storm-battered cottonwood trees paralleling the river, pausing in the shade of an old crippled cottonwood listing toward the water. He stopped near the middle of a patch of decimated thistle, their purple flower heads trampled by the flood waters. He relaxed the reins. The horse drank, noisily shook. Tracker leaned back in the saddle, eyes straight toward the sky. Just enough breeze. Cotton wisps floated like a lazy snowstorm. He reached out, trapping a piece of featherweight cotton, blew it into the dappled shade.

The Appaloosa's ears shot forward, hearing the sound before any human. At first, he thought it was music. A chant. Repetitive. He dismounted, looped the reins around a branch, moved toward the sound.

Izzie was slowly dancing around a small fire. *Atíva.* A dance in another world. Her face and body covered with black and white and yellow paint. A gray fox skin dangled from her neck. Legs bound with desert terrapin shells. Rattles. A *páho* prayer stick held in one hand. A golden eagle feather in the other.

She boiled water in a tin cup. Great energy radiated, surrounding her. She took out a four-inch bundle of *Ho'hoysi*, broke off a few sticks and leaves from the nervous stimulant, dropped them in. Waited to brew before she drank. After a few minutes she took another stick, placed it in an abalone shell and held it over the flames. The dry leaves caught. Smoke rose to send her message to *Túwanasavi*—the Center of the Universe.

Holding the eagle feather carefully, she used the underside, the side facing Mother Earth in flight, to brush the smoke in all six directions.

The direction of the smoke was critical.

East. The rising Sun and light for the soaring Eagle.

West. The Bear, to heal from within.

North. The Buffalo spirit. Wisdom and generosity.

South. The Coyote spirit. Service, family.

Looking up, she welcomed Father Sky and all that is masculine.

Looking down, to Mother Earth and all feminine spirits.

Brushing smoke over her heart, she begged for cleansing. To gain the ultimate peace. To rid herself of negative energy.

Tracker tensed, the hair on his neck twitched. Someone was watching him.

Izzie froze. Dropped the prayer stick. The eagle feather drifted away.

Someone was watching both of them. When he turned back toward her, she was gone.

26

Kate found Izzie crouched in a corner of the darkened apartment, rocking back and forth. She knelt beside her. Izzie was nude, smudged with paint, eyes glazed, arms stiff, palms up. Unaware of her surroundings.

Lamps broken, tables upside down, food on walls, pillow feathers drifting. Multiple self-inflicted lacerations. Bruises. Shortness of breath. Her face tense, hair matted, sweating. She brought her damp hands together like a bowl. Raised them as if making an offering to an unknown deity. Pluck cowered in the corner.

Suddenly, Izzie knocked Kate aside hard, sprang to her feet and ran out the door. She leapt over the railing, sprinted up the dirt road to the river at the western edge of the camp.

Kate was right behind, shoes hitting the ground hard.

Izzie's bare feet seemed to float above the rocks. Everything was quiet, absurdly serene. Izzie disappeared into the thick growth bordering the river. Blood pounded in her ears. Neck arched, defiant, outpacing Kate with her long strides.

Before going to headquarters, Tracker decided to head up to the south gate. A good place to gain perspective of the entire camp. Passed the swimming pool, sports field, followed the narrow track to the river. He dismounted, dropped the Appaloosa's reins. He tried to flex his right hand, but it still hurt like hell.

What did he just see? He blinked, re-focused. A nude woman in flight. The body seemed in midair. Suspended. Fractured light glinted on leafy branches, rocks, water, ferns. He sprinted toward her.

Izzie.

Angling his body and catapulting himself with all his strength, he collided with her, taking her down. Rolling. Clawing. Pulling on her torso. Her teeth clamped down on his neck. Wrenching one hand free, he twisted her head around, crunching her arms behind her in a vise-like grip. He pressed his full weight upon her, forcing her down. Pain shot down his leg.

Her fully exposed sclera went pure white, her body completely rigid. She convulsed. A white hand appeared in a flash, inserting a thin leather wallet into Izzie's mouth just before she swallowed her tongue. She gnashed her teeth into the leather, arms jerking violently. Every muscle in her body twitched, her stomach secreting acid.

On her knees, Kate's face was in Tracker's line of sight as he kept Izzie in a virtual body lock. Just as quickly as she inserted the billfold that saved Izzie's life, Kate withdrew a syringe from her pocket, edged off the tip, checked the flow. Hand steady as she bent forward, she injected the phenobarbital into Izzie's arm.

Izzie escaped into her private world. Eyes closed. Face full of sadness.

The grove was completely calm.

With a groan, Tracker rolled away. Rose to his knees. Kate leaned toward the slow-moving river, dipped her shirttail in the water. Dabbed it on Tracker's face, wiping blood from his nose, the bite on his neck. He was unable to speak.

Finally Kate said, "She's gone, in another place. She told me they were taking pictures of her soul. She hasn't eaten or drunk anything for days. I found her in the apartment, crouched in the corner in the dark. I locked her in, ran to the hospital for something, anything to calm her down. I tried to call you for help, but you had just left the camp."

He stiffly removed his shirt and helped Kate drape it around Izzie. He struggled to his feet and lifted her up. Cradling her. They followed Kate up the trail to the back of the nurses' quarters. Kate checked the quadrangle for staff, then motioned him inside. He placed Izzie on her bed. Kate pulled the sheets over her nude body.

"What now?" asked Tracker, completely drained.

"We wait."

27

Izzie finally opened her eyes, as if waking from a coma. A shudder. In a bare whisper, she said, "I want to sleep forever."

"Izzie." Kate said. "We'll take care of you. Whatever it is. Here, drink some tea."

"That German killed him," Izzie whispered.

Kate's hands went cold. Izzie pulled the sheets tightly around her. Now frozen in a fetal position.

Tracker turned to Kate. "What is she talking about? Killed him...?"

"She was in love," Kate whispered, backing out the door.

"Who was it?" Tracker asked. Kate avoided his eyes. "What's Izzie's story?"

"I know very little, but what I do know will break your heart. No wonder Izzie has cracked. She was chosen to be sent to a nursing school on a scholarship. By none other than the DAR. She was a Mennonite. Pennsylvania Hospital in Philadelphia. Army Nurse Corps."

She closed her eyes. "I'm a little sketchy on the rest of her family. They suffered terribly while she was gone." Kate started to cry.

Tracker pulled her to his chest, holding her gently, protectively. In a muffled voice, she said, "I wasn't truthful with you. I was worried you would take it wrong."

"Whoa. You can tell me anything."

"I think the man she was seeing was a cowhand on Grafton's ranch." She told Tracker that she warned Izzie to give him up. He was an outcast from the Mescalero reservation. It could never work. She kept Izzie's affair secret. Something very bad happened.

"Izzie told me that Klaus Schmidt followed them to a secret cave. Stabbed Carl in his heart. Raped Izzie. When he left the cave, she ran. And kept running."

Kate shivered. He kissed the top of her head.

"I saw her," said Tracker.

"What?"

"Go on, Kate, finish."

"When she got back to the cave, there was no trace of his body. She searched and searched. No tracks, nothing. What are you going to do now?"

He looked through the open bedroom door at Izzie, trying to imagine her pain, her shame. "I can't do anything for Carl. There is no corpse. His murderer is dead. I could never put Izzie on the stand. She has suffered too much already."

For now, he didn't want to do or say anything. Kate could keep her sedated. He would come up with an excuse.

Kate handed him his billfold, adding, "I'll see that you get a tetanus shot."

■■■

Tracker had to check out Izzie's story. He didn't doubt Izzie's claim that her lover's body was gone, but she was nearly hysterical at the time. Somehow he had to protect her. He dismounted at the cave entrance, looped the reins on a juniper branch. Ducked inside, allowing his eyes to adjust. A black mass streaked by his head, knocking off his hat. Three more flying bats swooped up, just missing him. The Appaloosa spooked, reared backwards, breaking the reins. He trotted away but stopped, looked back, eyes bulging. Tracker sat down, pulled out a handkerchief, wiped his face, hair, neck. He felt filthy.

A sudden cacophonous rush broke the silence. He swung around in time to see a massive bull elk crash through the trees. Being upwind, the stag was as startled as Tracker. All seven-hundred pounds barreled straight at Tracker. Head high, ears back, flared nostrils, the bull was close enough for Tracker to see the remnants of scrappy velvet still clinging to the antlers.

The bull curled back his lip, ground his teeth, enraged at possible harm to his harem. Tracker lunged to the side, trying to avoid the five-foot rack. He hit the ground hard. Elk bone ripped at his legs. A steel-like grip locked on his shoulders. Dragged him into the trees. The elk screamed, staggered into the forest. All Tracker could see were treetops, very tall pines. A face materialized inches from his own. Paul Chino.

"You scared the shit out of me."

"I tried to stop him, Mr. Dodds. *Wapiti* very fast." Tracker tried to get to his feet. His knees buckled. Paul raised him to a sitting position.

"It's time to talk," Paul said softly.

He said Albert Grafton was his father. He had an older half-brother, Carl Chino. Carl, like Paul, was a half-breed, sharing the same Apache mother, but Grafton wasn't his father. When their mother had fallen in

147

love with Grafton and became pregnant with his child, she had forbidden Carl to ever tell Albert that she had given birth to another son. His voice dropped as he explained that Carl Chino and Izzie Jahata were lovers.Izzie was Hopi. Carl was half-Apache, half-Mexican. A hopeless mixture from all sides. Paul knew they went to the cave to make love. When he saw Izzie streaking away, he knew something was wrong. He carried Carl's body to a higher spot, dug the grave.

"I buried him properly. Sealed the grave with rocks to keep the coyotes away. Then I snuck onto the reservation, burned his *wickiup*. All in one day. Carl is in the afterworld, the Land of Ever Summer, a paradise. I have told no one about this."

"Do you know who killed Carl?"

"I spotted a rider earlier that day, I'm certain it was Klaus Schmidt. He posted English-style. I saw him ride that way at the ranch."

So Paul had good reason to have murdered Klaus. He was certainly capable.

28

Izzie was prostrate, dull eyes on the ceiling. Trauma to her nervous system was palpable. Kate bathed her, dried her with warm towels. Treating scrapes, bleeding feet. She bathed Pluck, scrubbed the apartment. Finally she took a bath, careful to keep a loaded syringe of phenobarbital ready on the edge of the tub. With nothing to do but wait, she washed Tracker's shirt. Hung it on the doorknob to dry.

Izzie's fingers tightened on a wad of sheets. Tears welled in her eyes.

"Crying is okay," said Kate. "Crying is normal. What're you thinking? I've been going over everything you said, and there's no way you could have prevented Carl's murder."

"Whose shirt is that?" Izzie asked.

"Tracker's. I'll tell you all about that later. How about some of your tea?"

■■■

"Mr. T," J.C. said. "A note from Dr. Stillington."

Tracker read it quickly. "When?"

"An hour ago."

All the data from the state lab had finally arrived. He left immediately for Stillington's office.

Stillington looked up over his reading glasses. "I'll be with you in a moment."

At last Stillington said, "Thank you, Tracker. I don't know what I was thinking."

"I'm glad I was there to help."

"Can we keep this to ourselves?"

"Of course, Doctor."

"Finally, something definitive. I was really looking for some natural-occurring herbs, something a bit, if you will, mystical, insomuch as there was a scalping."

"And?"

"Nothing of the kind. The blood wasn't clotting because of the presence of warfarin sodium. Perhaps you know the drug better by the name Coumadin—it's around here. For rat control. And, medicinally as an anticoagulant, for clots caused by prolonged bed rest and immobility. An awful dilemma for my patients, always at risk of the bacteria eating through a lung artery, but clots are deadly."

Coumadin. Anyone could have given it to Schmidt. He could have accidently gotten some at the stables. "Are you sure there isn't something more specific—can't we narrow it down?"

"I talked to the state lab about other possibilities, they checked—nothing more."

"Well, that narrows the suspect list to the entire prison camp and the hospital."

"Maybe this might help a little. If the 'someone'—let's assume the victim didn't kill himself—knew a bit about the pharmacology of warfarin—a.k.a. Coumadin. They could give a dosage of the chemical knowing it would increase bleeding time significantly in a rather narrow time frame."

"Such as?"

"For discussion's sake—a push of fifty to seventy-five milligrams would cause a marked prolongation of bleeding time achieved, in say, thirty to thirty-six hours."

"Is that the only scenario?"

"No. Small doses over several days could accomplish the same results."

"Multiple doses would require multiple opportunities to administer the poison," said Tracker. The killer wouldn't be certain when the potentially lethal level would be reached. No, this was a one-dose deal. Schmidt didn't give it to himself—he was too smart, too clever to contaminate himself.

"There was one other thing that occurred to me," Stillington said.

The emergency alarm blared. Stillington hurried past Tracker, his white coat billowing. A ward patient was found on the floor in the shower. Water ran over his naked body. Bright red blood streamed from his mouth and nose, swirled down the drain.

Dr. Stillington turned off the shower. Knelt to check the carotid artery. No pulse. He rolled the patient face-up, pressed hard on the boney prominence above the eyes. No recoil, no pain response whatsoever. The patient was dead.

Stillington repeatedly pounded his fist on the wet tiles. Someone was gently pulling him to his feet. When he looked up he saw the terrified faces of a group of patients, one in a wheelchair, watching from the hallway.

"I've got you, Doc. Don't worry, I've got you," said Tracker.

"You are Chief Nurse, Kate!" Stillington was uncharacteristically sharp. "Where were you? Look at this chart, not one entry since you've been back on duty. Where were you?"

Kate couldn't speak. Izzie had become increasingly more manic, frenzied. Then not a word from her. Only complete silence.

Kate heard nothing that Dr. Stillington said until he shook her shoulders, his voice low and guarded, "You are fired."

∎∎∎

Kate unlocked the dead bolt. Izzie was up, backed into a corner.

Kate picked up the half-filled tea cup. "What's in this?"

Izzie sidestepped to her bedroom and slammed the door. Began screaming in Keresan. Stripping off her gown.

Kate felt for the syringe in her pocket. Checked the flow. Opened the door. The pins holding the window hinges were gone, the entire window casing on the rumpled bed. Izzie was gone.

All the way back to camp, Tracker kept thinking to himself that if whacked with seventy-five milligrams or more in one dose, Klaus was a dead duck. Any scrape, any small injury would have been fatal. Normal people don't bleed out and no one would have had the slightest reason to treat him for that. He needed to know more about the blood thinner. He started to turn back to the hospital. Standing on the swinging bridge, he realized he couldn't let anyone know what he was thinking. Hell, any one of his suspects could be the killer.

Suddenly it occurred to him, he had seen a large medical text at Grafton's house. He would ride cross-country, clear his mind.

Tracker dismounted, tied the reins to the hitching post. The air was heavy with moisture. He had to use both hands to wedge open the swollen door to the compound. Behind him, a steady voice called his name. Tracker's hand went to his pistol.

Paul held up his hands. "Mr. Grafton is in Ruidoso." He hesitated, then said, "I need help."

"What's up?"

"I just found a cow down. Looks like she's having trouble, it's her first calf. She's a kicker—I need some strong hands."

"Let's go."

Tracker followed Paul to the sun-drenched pasture behind the barn. Hard to keep up with him. They stopped short of the cow, both watching her every effort.

"I've seen this before, keep her steady. I need soap," said Tracker, rolling up his sleeves.

"In the bunkhouse," answered Paul, pointing at a long low adobe fifty feet away.

Tracker stepped over warbags, old magazines and dirty laundry between the bunks. Spotted a sink in the corner. He grabbed a scrap of soap. Lathered his hands and arms.

Tracker dropped to his knees. Paul took his cue, grabbed the cow's legs. Tracker lubricated the entrance to the birthing canal. Slid a hand in. "Head's turned back."

He worked for several minutes, pulling on the unborn calves' nose. Nothing moved. The cow was young and small. "No space," muttered Tracker. He jerked off his belt. With all his strength, he pushed the calf back inside the womb. The mother cow pushed against him, but Tracker won. He slid the belt around the calves' neck. Pulled with one hand while directing the nose with his other hand. The head came forward. Tracker grabbed the calf's front legs, eased the head out.

Paul swung around behind Tracker, checking for a prolapsed uterus. She was okay. "Good sign—she'll have more."

Tracker was sweated out. Mother and calf stable, he started for the bunkhouse.

"No, use my place," said Paul, gesturing toward a small unplastered adobe on the other side of the pasture. "I'll be there in a minute."

One-room home. Clean. Sparse. Two wood benches, a straight-back chair. Cot and small table. Bare plank floors. Two oil lanterns. No electricity. No toilet either. A chipped sink was adjacent to a wood-burning stove. Washing off, his eyes took in the corner shelves. Blue Ribbon flour. Pet milk. Arbuckle's coffee. Salt. Beans. Bundles of dried herbs. Mason jar filled with piñon nuts.

A sepia photograph in a simple black frame above the cot. Albert Grafton, looking straight at the camera. A woman wearing a stunning turquoise necklace was looking up at him, head tilted back. In love and vulnerable. Also full of Apache pride.

"My parents. Mr. Grafton's been a good father to me."

"You don't live in the main house?"

"My choice." Paul opened the iron stove. Prodded the ashes, stirring the banked coals. "Want something to drink? Coffee?" A puff of smoke permeated the room with the scent of piñon. "Maybe something stronger?"

Liquor was rarely available to Apaches, so Tracker was surprised, but then again, Paul wasn't on the reservation, so what the hell. "Sure."

Paul reached behind a wooden crate stacked neatly with kindling. Retrieved a short brown bottled with a rounded base. "I have an uncle in Oaxaca. Brings me a bottle every now and then. He always says, *"Para todo mal, mescal, y para todo bien, tambien."*

Tracker translated out loud. "For every ill, Mezcal, and for every good as well." He took the coffee mug offered by Paul. Strong, smoky flavor. Different than tequila. He liked it, and said so.

Paul replied, echoing Tracker's thoughts. "Stronger than tequila."

Tracker nodded, took another sip.

"The Spaniards named our tribe after mezcal. The Mescalero's."

"I didn't know that."

"One thing you sure do know about is cattle, Mr. Dodds."

"I grew up on a ranch in Kansas. Haven't worked cattle for years though."

"You had a good teacher."

"My father didn't allow room for mistakes."

They stepped outside. Tracker slipped on his dark glasses. He knew better than to stare at an Apache, so he lowered his eyes and asked, "You know, Izzie's told me about Carl. You look after her pretty close." Paul said nothing. Tracker took a sip, liked the kick. The liquor had emboldened him.He turned a bit toward Paul and said cautiously, "A few days ago I accidently came upon Izzie way out in nowhere. She was praying. I got a strange feeling someone else was there, too." He emptied his mug. "Never have figured out who the third person was watching, Izzie or me."

"You're living up to your name. Izzie was beginning the purification dance—her own ceremony for Carl. For some reason she stopped."

Tracker looked out over the pasture toward a patch of shade, the mother cow was standing over her newborn. "Animals have instincts, just like us. We like to see things through. You know, to completion."

"That is what she was doing. Performing a sacred ritual for Carl. We are responsible for keeping spiritual and physical life in harmony with Nature. In life, and in death."

"I understand."

"Yes, I think you do. Tell me, Mr. Dodds, if you found out Izzie was part of the murder in the camp—I'm not saying she was—what would you do?"

"Right now, Izzie is a very sick lady. Very sick in her mind. I came out here to see if I could look up something in Mr. Grafton's library."

"The door's open, Mr. Dodds. After what you've done to help, I'm sure he would want you to use his library."

Tracker walked quickly through the series of rooms to the book-shelves. Running his eyes along the books, he found it. *A General Medical Text: Diagnosis & Treatment.* There it was in the index: Conditions of bleeding and clotting. Graphs, diagrams, chemicals which could interfere with another.

BISHYDROXYCOUMARIN.

"Coumarin," he said aloud. Second cousin to Coumadin. He understood very little. The compound diagrammed required 24 to 72 hours, depending on the dosage, to become fully active, to prevent the necessary step in a chain of events to form a clot. First, it went to work on the liver. Out of sight. Secondly, the effects went on for 24 to 96 hours after the last dose—or single-load dose—was given. Finally—a conclusive time span.

At the front door, he realized Paul had left him alone in the house.

31

Deep in a trance, like a sphinx, Izzie focused her entire being on the sacred ritual. Oblivious to her surroundings, she sat erect, her hair hanging loose over her naked body. She began chanting. No subjects, no verbs.

The Hopi way. *Powamu. Pavásio.*

Purification. A relief of sorrow. Praying for Carl's *hikwsi*, his breath, to move to another place, the Lower World. To another form of existence, knowing that his *hikwsi* would return as clouds or rain, *katsinam*. She was also praying for more.

She rose slowly, moving rhythmically around the pole, prayer stick and eagle feather in hand. It was almost over.

■■■

He passed the juncture of the Bonito and Rio Ruidoso going west. From what Kate had told him, he was close to where Izzie often went. The Appaloosa needed rest. He pulled to a stop in a stand of ponderosa, knowing the road would peak out soon. He guessed it would take him another thirty minutes to get back to camp. Then he heard the first in a series of cries. He pulled out his binoculars, focused. Below him, he thought he saw Izzie inside a natural-occurring rock amphitheater. How did she get out?

Izzie's dancing was much more crazed than before. He adjusted the focus again, it couldn't be what he thought he was seeing. This wasn't about cleansing or purification, or getting rid of negative energy.

On top of the pole was a scalp.

32

J. C., Maxwell, and several guards huddled together on the headquarter steps. J. C. looked mad as hell.

Tracker reined in his horse. Didn't dismount. "What's gone wrong now?"

"Müeller escaped. After lunch."

"Noon?" A glance at his watch. "I suppose you've done an extensive search, questioned everyone, including the captain?"

"Yes, sir. We know one thing—he was last seen over at the stables." Tracker surveyed the chain-link fence topped with coiled razor wire. "No horses missing, Mr. T. He's on foot, should be easy for you to track him. I've seen you track from the air—if you can spot the invisible trail from a low-flying plane, you sure as hell can track him..."

"I'm not going after the sonofabitch," snapped Tracker.

"What?"

"Müeller's off federal property. Let the sheriff get him. I've got more important things to do."

...

Stillington had left orders that he was not to be disturbed. Tracker thought he recognized the nurse on duty, but was unsure. He took a seat in the empty waiting area. White metal chair. Paint chipped. He tossed a stack of very old, tattered magazines on the floor, propped up his leg. It dawned on him. She was the postmistress. He waited, irritable, stuck. What had he just witnessed? His brain sizzled like an iron skillet full of bacon. He forced himself to detach. Thinking of bacon, he nodded off, chin down. Footsteps awakened him an hour later. He focused on the blurry image at the nurse's station.

"Where the hell is Kate?" Tracker growled.

Not looking up, Stillington said, "I've dismissed them."

"Both of them?"

"Both." He didn't explain and didn't look like he wanted to hear another word about them. He pointed in the direction of their quarters. "You know where they live."

...

No answer at the door. He used the flat of his hand. Struck the door hard. "It's me, Izzie got out somehow."

Kate opened the door. "She came back. She's in bad shape. "

Izzie appeared wearing a white terrycloth robe and sat on the sofa. She had bathed. Washed hair combed back. Tracker pulled a straight-backed chair over, took her hand. Her eyes glued on his. Not a blink.

"I've been so worried about you. Izzie, I saw you." She withdrew her hand from his light grasp.

"I saw prayer sticks. An eagle feather in your hand. All very important to you." Her hands closed, her knuckles white. He waited a moment. "You are grieving for someone. My heart goes out to you. But, there was something else, Izzie, there was a pole.

"On top of that pole—Izzie, look at me—on top of that pole was an object, a part of a human being. Part of a human scalp."

Izzie stood abruptly. Slapped him hard.

"A blond-haired scalp."

"Yes!" screamed Izzie. "Yes!" Her eyes widened, irises sparking like flames. "I told you he killed Carl."

Kate stood, but Tracker motioned her to stay back. "You killed Schmidt, didn't you?" Izzie stood frozen and silent. "You killed Schmidt," Tracker repeated.

"Yes." She sat down. "I killed him."

"Not true," said Kate, barely audible.

"Quiet, Kate, let her talk."

"I'm not about to stay quiet."

He turned to Izzie. "How did you kill him?"

"Poison—an overdose—Coumadin from the hospital pharmacy. Because he..." Her mouth moved but there was no sound, no words.

"Please, Izzie, tell me everything. I need to know."

"I told you." She spoke in rapid bursts. Barely breathing in air. "Carl and I would meet up out of sight. Had to be careful. We were on a blanket just inside the cave. Schmidt jumped Carl, tied him up. Made him watch. He raped me. Then he killed Carl." She finally took a breath. Her voice nearly inaudible, she said, "When I went back, his body was gone."

"I want you to know that Paul Chino buried Carl properly."

Tears flowed down Izzie's reddened face. She looked feverish. She clasped both hands above her head, looked upward, mouthing words over and over.

It was painful to watch. Tracker hated his job, but he had to ask. "How did you poison him?"

Izzie's words poured out. Schmidt had been a sick man when they brought him to the hospital. Pneumonia. Then a ruptured gall bladder. Gallstones. Tremendous pain. He really couldn't keep anything down. But no matter how nauseated, he craved the sourdough bread from the hospital cafeteria. Hard-crusted. One of the cooks had a starter, it was her specialty.

She retreated, halting her story. Reverted to her nurse's training. Coumadin was bitter when administered straight. Patients were given fruit juice after Coumadin treatment to cut the aftertaste. It was easy to mix the crystalline substance with butter, spread it on the bread. She had the opportunity. Dr. Stillington sent either her or Kate to the camp every few days to do follow-ups. It was State law.

"Is that when you gave him the poisoned bread?"

"Two days before you got here."

"Why then?"

"It was the last time I was sent over. Klaus was back working with the horses. Germans like strange tastes, sour pickles, cheese that stinks. It was easy to get him to eat the bread."

"I don't believe a word you've said, Izzie." Kate started to cry. "Why are you lying?"

"I'm going to have to arrest you, Izzie, you know that, don't you?"

"No," snapped Kate. She grabbed Tracker with both hands on his forearms.

"I have no choice. You both know it."

"Tracker, listen to me. Listen," Kate said flatly. "He raped me. I killed him."

"When did he rape you?"

"At the stables, weeks ago." She released her hands. Tracker's shirt-sleeves were damp, crumpled from her grip. "I killed him the day you arrived."

"Where?"

"At the swimming pool. I was getting a sample."

Tracker blew out. Cleared his throat. "How did you go about getting a sample?"

"A chest needle. It's very long. Have you seen one?"

"I have."

Izzie was watching them both. Eyes wide, darting between them. Her breathing uneven. She twitched. Stored-up anguish and loss threatened to explode.

Kate took a step back and turned away. When she turned around, she looked feverish. Sweat on her upper lip and brow. With difficulty, she said, "I didn't plan it. I was kneeling at the side of the pool. Schmidt must have followed me. He grabbed me from behind. Dragged me into the storage room. Started ripping off my uniform. I took that needle. Jammed it into his belly until I felt bone."

Kate turned to Izzie. Pleading. Begging her to understand. She was guilty, the needle had killed him.

"No, Kate. I did it. I was grieving. I wanted revenge. The scalp is my token."

Quiet. A long silence. Exhaustion permeated the air.

Finally, in a controlled voice, Tracker said, "I've got to think this out. Both of you stay here. Got it? Don't talk to anyone. Just...please stay here until I get back."

33

Kate and Izzie sat in silence, numbed by equal admissions of guilt. Each felt such self-image degradation. Neither had confided in the other. Not a word about rape. Such humiliation. Nothing was said of the cauterizing terror each woman experienced.

Kate whispered, "What now?"

Izzie looked up, saying, "I don't know."

"He is a lawman. We both admitted we were guilty of murder." Kate understood now what Izzie meant when she had said she wanted to sleep forever.

The words, coated with loathing, slowly spilled out from Kate. "I had just come back from riding. Asked him to unsaddle my horse. I turned my back on him, and..."

"He was very strong,"

"Filthy bastard!"

Schmidt had stripped her. He was like a demented monster. Dragged her through the manure, dumped her behind the silos. Left her unconscious.

"Mary Rogers, from the laundry, found me by the back door. She picked me up, bathed and dressed me in clean clothes, just like I was a child. I remember smelling soap and hiss of steam." Kate's face contorted under the pressure of the memory.

"I didn't want my body anymore. He took away my intimacy, my confidence, my self-worth. Left me angry, tired, empty. Empty," Kate said, barely perceptible to the ear.

Izzie sensed it. Not being one who shows affection, her hand on Kate's shoulder was a gesture of massive importance. Izzie spoke quietly, but more firmly than she had for weeks. "In our life on the Three Mesas, we have what we call *koyaanisqatsi*. It is a place, a society of evil. Immorals. Degenerates. I swore revenge. I put him in that society forever."

Kate dampened a dish towel, handed it to Izzie. Did the same for herself. Took a deep breath. One thing had not been explained completely.

"Izzie, what about the scalp? You told Tracker it was your trophy."

"First I am a woman, but, I am Hopi woman. You will not understand, think I am crazy. I scalped him. It was my duty. I had to. My plan was to wait until the blood thinner was at maximum, then attack him. I went to the camp, checked the stables.

"I didn't have anything worked out," Izzie continued, "But I planned to stab him with something, anything to make the bastard bleed. Stick him in the belly, watch him die as his blood poured into his abdomen. But, he wasn't there."

"That was the day Tracker arrived."

"Yes, late that afternoon. J.C. told me he was going to El Paso to pick up the new Inspector in Charge, so I knew I had to find that bastard. I was afraid the new inspector might stop us -- medical personnel -- from going inside the compound." Izzie put the kettle on the stove. "I headed back to the hospital, on the south trail, by the pool. No one was around, most of the men were still eating. I heard something. I wasn't sure what it was. I opened the door to the little supply room."

"A big enough room to screw someone," said Kate.

"He was on the floor, clutching his belly. I watched him die. It wasn't enough. Maybe I was crazy, but I knew what I had to do. I wanted revenge—I had to get revenge for Carl. Take his scalp. Release his evil spirit. His soul.

"I picked up a paint scraper—I had seen the men use it to clean the pool gutters—I chiseled off his scalp."

She dropped the bundle of Hopi tea into a crockery teapot. "I didn't see the wound in his belly. I dragged him to the pool, pushed him in. I pulled my skirt down, dragged it over my tracks. Men started coming out of the mess tent. Grafton's truck was parked inside the compound. I hid under a tarp. When he drove away, I slipped out. Walked home."

Kate wrapped her arms around Izzie, tears flowing down her cheeks. "We'll figure a way out," she whispered. "What we need is your tea. Better yet, we need rum. In one of those beautiful glasses I brought back from Wyoming."

Five glasses, that's all those kind church people had not pillaged. Her mother would die all over again if she knew Kate had them. Her hands shook as she poured a measure of rum into each glass. Fumbled with the cork. Almost spilled the glass she handed to Izzie.

Why hadn't Tracker arrested them on the spot?

34

J.C. stuck his head in Tracker's office. "Morning, Mr. T, you okay?"

"I'm good," Tracker lied. "Bring some tea, the canister Izzie gave me."

J.C. set the thick ceramic mug on Tracker's desk, commenting that he was surprised that the tea was naturally sweet. No response from him, Tracker was absorbed in thought. J.C. cleared his throat. No response. "Well, Mr. T, I'll just go sharpen my pencil."

Tracker smiled but didn't let J.C. see it. He blew on the hot tea. His breath crystalized in the early morning chill. He rubbed his hands together. Slammed his fist hard on the desktop. Tea sloshed all over the notebook and desktop. J.C. was quick with a towel.

"Shit!" Tracker ripped the notebook in half, threw it in the wastebasket. "Not relevant. Not relevant at all." He stood, hands on hips, arched his back. Stretched. He was about to explode. He had managed to suppress his rage in front of the girls.

"Hey, Mr. T," J. C. said, "Calm down. Relax." Tracker closed his eyes, clinched his fists. J.C. realized he was on the edge of losing it. "I ran into Paul this morning when I was dropping Linda off at my sister's. He said you're pretty good at delivering calves."

A change in subject. Let his brain cool. A long minute passed before he answered. "Done a few."

"He said you just took over."

"Not quite. That cow was really agitated, kicking and all. I watched how Paul handled her, calmed her down, got control of her legs. Couldn't just stand there gawking, so I did the delivery part. Couldn't have handled it without Paul controlling her."

"He approved of what you did, saving the calf, the momma, too."

"Anything going on your end, J. C.?"

"As a matter of fact. Paul was pretty friendly, thanks to you. He said he saw Müeller."

"Where? When?"

"Yesterday—late. Paul said he was out looking for a couple of strays, up near San Patricio. That's where he saw him."

"Did he make contact?"

"No, you know Paul, he just watched. J. C. explained how he had seen the sheriff's car and flagged him down, telling Halligan about the sighting. "Old Halligan actually smiled at me."

Tracker said only, "Good."

"Time for roll call, Mr. T." He started for the door, then added, "You wanted to talk to me?"

"You've told me what I was going to ask."

"One other thing—Halligan got talkative," said J. C. "Told me Álvarez tore up the Rusty Anchor last night. He has him in jail in Carrizozo. Pretty beat up."

"Good."

His third 'good' for the morning.

After J. C. left, Tracker retrieved the note pad. Tore out his notes. Slid them in his pocket.

He was about to leave when there was a knock on his door. An unfamiliar rapid tapping. "Who is it?"

Dr. Stillington stepped into the office. "I'm taking water samples. Thought I might drop by."

"Glad you're here. Have you found a new charge nurse yet, Doctor?"

"Not new. I brought Kate back. I had a long talk with her. You don't know this, but on Kate's watch prior to my relieving her, she was paying no attention to her duties. A patient died, I believe needlessly."

Tracker felt sick. "What did she tell you that changed your mind?"

"Kate really took her mother's death badly." The doctor repeated her story of the looting of the home, the long-time difficulties with her mother. Plus, filled with worry over Izzie. Izzie seemed to have slid into her native background, possibly even used hallucinatory herbs. "I told her to keep me up to date on her progress. If she needs help to let me know. I'm off now. Got to see a patient in Carrizozo."

In the quiet of his office, Tracker stood at the window. He knew the good doctor didn't drop by to tell him about staff problems. No, Stillington was no fool. Stillington had a problem. His own good conscience. No co-incidence Stillington kept bottles in every drawer. He had his demons and needed the liquor to survive. How much does he know? Tracker headed to the door, called out to the doctor, "By chance, are you headed down to see Álvarez?"

"Yes, why do you ask?"

It didn't take much to get information from the doctor. Stay away from medical privacy issues and he'd tell you anything, especially if Doc found it amusing. Stillington knew all about his next patient, the one in jail. A long-time 'business arrangement' existed between his old friend Grafton and the County Clerk. On one of Stillington's more memorable house calls, one that Álvarez loved to talk about in public, he had treated Álvarez's swollen testicles, the result of an encounter with a black widow spider in his own outhouse. Though the clerk was in terrible pain, he was more concerned about missing a closing with Grafton at the courthouse. Álvarez didn't spread that part of his story around. He had admitted to Dr. Stillington that he damn well knew every single one of Grafton's land takeovers hurt honest, good people, and he was well compensated for ensuring it all looked legal. Tracker dropped heavily in his chair. Clear as can be, he thought. Stillington and Grafton were old friends. The doctor delivered Grafton's son. But the doctor wasn't tied up in illegal land swindles.

35

He had sorted through every fact, shuffled and reshuffled. Still couldn't deal out a solution. There was no conspiracy. Each girl had acted on their own. Therefore, they were equally guilty. Why didn't he arrest them? Or tell the sheriff to bring them in?

Both raped by the same man—a vicious animal. However, his murder was the task of a court to grapple with. Times were rife with hardship, loss, not to mention a world at war. The legal system was overwhelmed. Would the court, the jury rightly adjudicate the case? Damn-it-all-to-hell. They were both guilty of murder.

Almost dark. Sky deep indigo, a velvet-like blanket of saturated color enveloped the canyon. A car crossed the bridge, lights bounced on the dirt road to the camp. Halligan and Paul Chino.

Tracker saw the flash of light, went to the door. "Christ, what now?" he said aloud.

The sheriff pried himself from the car. "Good evening, Sheriff." Tracker remained above on the landing.

"Dodds, got a minute?"

"Sure thing, what can I do?"

"Paul called me. Big trouble at the Grafton ranch."

"What's up?"

"He won't let me see anything. Won't talk 'til you're with us."

"Let's go." Tracker crawled into the back seat, tapped Paul on the shoulder. Some people, especially Indians, can hide every emotion—no body language, no eye contact. Paul was an expert—he didn't give away a thing. The hour's drive to the ranch was long and silent. It might have given Tracker time to think through his quandary, except for Halligan's erratic driving. The sheriff was a jabber—hitting the brakes, swerving, jabbing the brakes, speeding up, only to hit the brakes again. Tracker couldn't get out of the car fast enough when they finally reached the ranch.

Paul led them in, carefully sidestepping shards of broken pottery. The body of Albert Grafton lay face up next to the piano. Blood pooled around his head, a crude stick protruded from the bottom of his jaw. The weapon had ruptured the sublingual artery and buried itself in the man's tongue.

Even before he knelt by the body, Tracker recognized the primitive implement as one of Grafton's prized prayer sticks. The prayer stick, which once had been used in a ceremony to blow life into an infant. Now used to kill.

"This is not the act of an Indian," said Paul. He looked at Tracker, pleading with his eyes. "No Indian is that disrespectful. A knife, bare hands, yes."

Halligan walked slowly around the body. Grafton had put up a fight, consistent with his demeanor, but he hadn't been quick enough. He knew Paul was a half-breed, and had heard the rumors that Grafton was the father, but the sheriff always thought Grafton treated Paul as paid help, making him live outside the main house. Had things become too much, too unbearable for Paul? Halligan started to speak, but stopped at the sight of Tracker's raised hand.

"I'm sorry to say this, Paul, but it occurred to me that Mr. Grafton just might have had some enemies that he coerced one way or another to sell him their land," said Tracker. "Did he ever work on any cases dealing with land grants?"

36

Hands deep in his pockets, Sheriff Halligan walked aimlessly back and forth in the darkness outside the main gate of Grafton's house. Too much, he kept thinking, too much pressure piled on him. It had been two days since he received the telephone call from the Attorney General in Santa Fe, advising him that there was going to be a full investigation of his office. His plight was alluded to in an article in yesterday's *Albuquerque Journal*:

> Lincoln County is again rife with illegal activity. Only a few decades ago, the country had reeled under the violence of the Lincoln County Wars. Now it is home to real estate grabs by lawyers wise to the ways of Spanish/Mexican Land Grants. With full cooperation from the law, a group of political honchos from around the state have become some of the wealthiest and largest landowners in the United States.

Halligan had hardly heard a word said inside the house except for Tracker's mention of *land grants*. For damn sure a lynching mob was gathering. Otherwise known as a hunt for a scapegoat.

Or maybe not. Halligan stopped pacing—Dodds is right. Grafton was deeply involved in the corruption, and now he's dead. If he could solve this murder, and the one which took place at the internment camp, he might get the AG off his back. He strode quickly back inside to the crime scene, already formulating his plan.

37

Halligan looked at Paul standing stoically behind the roped-off area several feet away from the body. Yellow evidence markers dotted the crime scene.

"Well, I'll be—it all makes sense," said the sheriff. "I think you could be right, Dodds. I've got it. Müeller's on the loose. And, he's short—he struck Grafton from below, then he finished the job by clunking him on the head with the pot. Hey, didn't your man, J. C., say Müeller was close to the dead man, Klaus Schmidt?"

The notion was the sheriff's, thought Tracker. Let him keep going.

"Until now, Dodds, I've been thinking you shoved this manhunt off on me for some tom-fool ulterior motive. Thought it would make me feel important if I brought back your runaway, something like that." Thinking out loud, Halligan cast out a thought, saying, "Suppose that Müeller knew what Grafton was doing, and tried to blackmail him. He wanted more, lots more. "Paul, don't touch anything. I'll send my team. Don't slip away. This isn't over. Come on, Dodds, I've got to get back."

▪▪▪

"Just heard something over the shortwave," J. C. said, stepping into the office, wondering if he should tell Tracker. "Mr. T, months ago we happened on to the sheriff's wavelength. Kind of like to listen in now and then."

"You heard something?" Tracker was standing at the window, looking out over the darkened camp.

"Müeller was caught at Álvarez's house. He was snuggled up with the old lady since her man's in jail."

"Did you hear any charges the sheriff has made?"

"Arrested him for the murder of Grafton."

Tracker spun around so quickly he made J. C. jump back. He seemed to hold his breath for a moment. He made up his mind. "And Müeller murdered Schmidt, too."

"Schmidt—Mr. T...?"

"Müeller was his runner, his go-fer. You know damn well Klaus used him, cheated him, right? Good enough motive for me. The scalping is a red herring—he scalped him to shift blame to an Indian."

J. C. nodded. "It makes sense. Not a completely bad assumption. Müeller watched the money going to Schmidt. Grafton, too." He leaned forward, hands on the desk, tapping his wedding ring on the wooden surface. "But..."

"But what, J.C.?"

"What about procedure? Mr. T, do your job. Do you have enough proof?"

"It's the sheriff's job." Tracker unbuttoned his top button, loosened his tie.

"Do you know something that you're not telling me? Are you holding something back?" Tracker avoided his eyes. "Mr. T, you can't hold back."

"The Sheriff said something smart."

"You cannot do this."

"The objective is—the bigger picture—it's a wrap. And no one is hurt."

"What about Daehne? Will he buy it?"

"I don't give a shit about Daehne." Tracker's voice was low, almost a growl.

"What about the men? I'm with the patrolmen every day. You're not. I know what they think, and who they would believe."

"Are you saying they would believe you before they believed me?"

"Look, Mr. T, I'm not talking about obedience. In my little pueblo of Tortugas, we make a pilgrimage every December to celebrate the Feast of Our Lady of Guadalupe. My mother got up very early, climbed the rocky trail up Tortugas Mountain until she couldn't anymore. I never thought to question her."

"What is your point? Bless your mother, but isn't that all about blind obedience?"

"Or guilt?" J. C. responded, as a question.

"Sit your ass down. ¡Siéntate! We'll talk about justice."

"She is not making a deal with God," J.C. snapped. "You are a helluva good border patrol officer." A wry smile crossed Tracker's face. "What you're up to could amount to breaking the law."

Dr. Stillington suddenly appeared in the doorway to Tracker's office. "At ease, gentlemen. I was waiting outside and couldn't help but hear you both frothing at the mouth. Perhaps we all should discuss what we know."

"What I know is that Müeller is a monster," A blood vessel in Tracker's neck pulsed. "Schmidt, too."

"You are in a tough spot, Agent Dodds," said Stillington.

"Goddamnit! Rules! Justice? No justice for Schmidt carving out Maria's face. He killed Paul's brother. Raped both Kate and Izzie."

J.C. opened his mouth, but was speechless. It was the doctor's turn to surprise both of them. "I agree. I have no qualms. Are Kate and Izzie cold-blooded killers? No. They are victims."

38

Late Monday evening he visited the girls. Kate was on her break, checking on Izzie. They were both skittish, like high-strung racehorses. "Come in, I'll fix you a drink," Kate said. "I only have a couple of minutes before I have to get back."

"No thanks, maybe later. Let's take a walk. Get some fresh air—it'll be good for Izzie."

The threesome walked slowly through the cottonwoods down to the river. The Rio Bonito gurgled innocently. He put his arms around both girls, pulled them close.

"This is complicated," said Tracker.

"We know," said Kate, her voice breaking. "And it's our fault." Near tears, she ran her hand through her cropped hair. "Isn't it, Izzie?"

Izzie's brow creased with worry. At least her eyes seemed focused. She was listening. "I did it. You did it, too. We both killed him."

Tracker abruptly stopped them. "We will never say those words again. To no one. Not out loud, or in your heart. Never. Listen carefully." He waited a moment—looking at the two broken women. If he snapped his fingers, either of them might disintegrate. "I'm sorry—but I have to tell you something. Mr. Grafton is dead. He was killed—murdered by an escaped prisoner, Gerhardt Müeller. The cook at the camp.

"I just heard that Sheriff Halligan has him under arrest. Müeller has been charged for the murder of Mr. Albert Grafton." Both girls stepped back. Tension crackled in the air. He was careful not to move, or they might run. He coughed, licked his lips, and said, "And the murder of Seaman Klaus Schmidt."

Kate and Izzie looked at each other. This was too much to comprehend. Both women stood stiffly, arms at their sides. Izzie closed her eyes, crying softly.

Finally Kate spoke. Tears rolled down her cheeks, unheeded. "Are you going to straighten the sheriff out?"

"The sheriff's correct, he's got it right. Do you both understand me?"

"You're not going to tell him the truth?" Kate asked in a whisper.

Tracker shook his head. "In the real world, we know who killed whom, but—BUT—in the just world, and there's currently precious little justice, Schmidt killed himself with the kind of vile life he led."

Tracker took Izzie's hand, brought Kate under his arm. Glints of moonlight sparkled off quiet eddies in the river. Tall timothy grasses barely moved, tassels blinking like eyelashes. Together they walked back to the nurse's quarters.

The living room of the apartment felt larger, the lamplight brighter. Pluck wagged his tail, thumping the couch.

"Thank you, Tracker Dodds. You have saved my life. I am very tired. Good night," said Izzie, softly shutting the door to her bedroom.

"I'll have that drink," Tracker said. "Kate, you be the nurse you are. Get Izzie well. Help her rejoin life."

39

Tracker managed some sleep after the sheriff dropped by to say he had spoken to Chief Vonshooven in El Paso, highly praising Dodds and clearing him of all charges. With rare politeness, Halligan suggested informing Captain Daehne that Seaman Müeller was in custody, and would face a trial. An attorney would be provided. He advised caution.

After J.C. returned from delivering the captain back to the camp, he asked Tracker how the meeting had gone. Tracker told him the captain was stoic, no surprise. But Daehne had added the fact that many in the camp, including himself, thought Müeller was guilty from the start.

As had been his practice since his arrival almost a month ago, he asked for his horse. J.C. waited outside headquarters holding the reins of the Appaloosa. He gave Tracker a lift up, checked the breast collar. The horse fought the bit, tossed his head, jerked backwards. "He's all yours. Hope you can handle him today. Feeling his oats, Mr. T."

"I think I can run some of his energy out of him."

"Well, if he shows up rider less, he's mine from then on."

Tracker spun the horse to the south, calling out, "Get back to your pencils."

His bad leg was quiet, his hand better. The rhythmic stride, pounding hooves, the sheer elegance of the gelding put Tracker at peace. Sun still below the horizon. Pale ambient light gaining warmth. He saw a rider approaching, instinctively knew it was Kate.

"Dr. Stillington let me off for the day. He said I'd been on duty much too long lately. How about I ride with you?"

"Anything you want."

Kate clucked to her mare, who fell into step with the Appaloosa. "Everyone's talking about how expertly you delivered that calf. Are you sure you want to always be a border patrol officer?"

"Not necessarily, but it's my lot. Once I had a dream, like all us optimists."

Kate chuckled. "You optimistic? You're too tough on yourself to be optimistic."

"Really, Kate, I could see myself with my own ranch. I'd run it well. But..."

Note From the Author

For several years, I lived with Native Americans, serving as a physician. My patients were from numerous tribes in northwestern New Mexico, including Hopi, Zuni, Laguna, Navajo and Apache. Out of curiosity, I inquired about their various rituals, including the purification and scalp dances. The stories I was told are confirmed by the exhaustive writings of Frank Waters, *Book of the Hopi*, as well as articles from the *47th Annual Report of the Bureau of American Ethnology of the Smithsonian.*

I hold the Native American in highest esteem, and respectfully ask you, the reader, to accept depicted rituals as a composite of the available (and rare) descriptions.

My heartfelt thanks to the former New Mexico Secretary of Cultural Affairs, Mr. Stuart Ashman, for arranging visits to Fort Stanton, the intact hospital, living quarters, and the off-limits remains of the internment camp, including the swimming pool built by the German POWs.

My personal thanks also to Dr. Helga DeLisle, Joseph P. Hammond, J.D., J. T. Prichard, DVM, Dr. Maryce M. Jacobs, and Dr. James J. McBride.

Readers Guide

1. The POW camp at Fort Stanton became a model for incarceration in the United States. How did the status of non-combatant aliens, such as the distressed seamen from the *Columbus,* change after Pearl Harbor?

2. Before the U.S. entered the war, the prisoners were allowed to roam the countryside around Fort Stanton and neighboring villages. Is this surprising to you today?

3. The border patrol is empowered by the Department of Justice. Any thoughts as to why the border patrol was given the task to enforce POW camps in the US during WWII?

4. Discuss Captain Daehne's reason for scuttling his ship, the *Columbus.* What role did the *USS Tuscaloosa* play?

5. How was Tracker qualified for enrollment in the Border Patrol at Camp Chigas? Remember that agents must be bilingual.

6. Using his experience as a cadet and as a barnstormer, Tracker also qualified as a pilot for the border patrol. Was this advance in rank, coupled with his injuries, the probable reason Chief Vonshooven assigned Tracker to Fort Stanton?

7. Izzie's family suffered greatly during WWII. Discuss the delicate uniqueness of the Hopi at that time in history.

8. Blacks in the armed forces were segregated during WWII. The mood in New Mexico was quite different. How so?

9. New Mexico was rife with land-grabbing crooks at the turn of the century, with savvy lawyers stealing land from desperate settlers and Hispanic Land Grant owners. Is this practice still going on today?

10. Tuberculosis was rampant in the U.S. at this time. Why was the Merchant Marine hospital built in such a remote area?

11. Was this extremely dangerous disease portrayed convincingly through Dr. Stillington's handling of patients and his medical acumen?

12. The New Mexico Department of Health required mandatory testing of the water supply and the swimming pool. Nurses and

border patrolmen moved freely inside the POW camp. Did this arrangement emphasize both the possibility of physical endangerment as well as the possibility of contagion?

13. Despite Dr. Stillington's problems with liquor, was he still a sympathetic character?

14. Was the poker game setting in Juarez and the environment of the U.S.-Mexican international border convincing? Did the resulting commendations for Tracker and J.C. ring true?

15. Does Tracker's telling the story of his broken leg, hospital stay and progressive recovery seem real to you? The flood and Beaver's death took a toll on his body. But as the book progressed, did you feel that Tracker was recovering?

16. Kate's poor relationship with her estranged mother and her two divorces hardened her. Do you feel gradual changes in her attitude toward Tracker? Did you want to cheer when the judge ruled in Kate's favor in Wyoming? How about the aerobatics?

17. A more serious question: Did you understand the lack of a clotting mechanism?

18. Did you find Klaus Schmidt's disturbing family background convincing? Convincing enough to torture Maria?

19. The Hopi tea serves as a soothing concoction native to New Mexico, but it has nothing to do with the underlaying theme of the mystery. Kent Jacobs wrote about justice. Do you think justice was served? Should the girls have been charged for murder? Kate may have gotten away with self-defense, but Izzie? Did it surprise you that Dr. Stillington was in full agreement with Tracker? Was J.C. in the right for challenging Tracker's motive?

20. Fort Stanton and the Merchant Marine Hospital exist today, saved as a New Mexico Historical Site by an adaptive reconstruction as a living history center. The German POW camp across the Bonito River hasn't faired as well, but the empty shell of the German swimming pool remains in the shadow of Sierra Blanca. Find out more about this beautiful area: www.fortstanton. com and www.NMHistoricSites.org. Both websites current at the time of the publication of this book.